CHARADE

Jade C. Jamison

CHARADE

No kissing necessary. Definitely no sex.

Erica Larson had dreamed of being a lawyer for as long as she could remember, but the job at Ford & Associates—a family business run by a father and his three sons—is sheer drudgery. Erica is ready to pull up stakes and move home—until devilishly handsome but arrogant Brock Ford, the youngest son, makes her an offer she can't refuse.

Play his fiancée for a month...maybe two, because his future with the firm depends on deception.
Just attend a function here and there.
No kissing and definitely no sleeping together.

Well...maybe one kiss.
Or two.

And, before Erica knows it, she's doubting if she can distinguish between fiction and reality, because her heart can no longer tell the difference. Can she stop herself from becoming a victim of his charm before it's too late?

Copyright

CHAPTER ONE

BROCK FORD RESISTED the urge to clench his jaw—for the tenth time during this short meeting.

It was a habit he'd broken in the courtroom, in the bedroom, on the green, and even standing in a long line, but it was always a behavior he reverted back to when surrounded by family in a tense situation. His father Brady Ford had until recently been a hard ass, demanding and unforgiving, and as the youngest of three boys, Brock had learned to keep his tongue in check. The only way to do that was to clench his jaw so he could ensure his mouth was closed and not flippantly spewing out his true thoughts.

He'd learned that lesson at eight years old to avoid a spare-the-rod spanking, and it had continued through high school when he'd clamped his jaw down instead of telling the football coach to fuck off. It was that kind of self-taught self-control that had earned him the position of starting quarterback then and, by college, his clenched jaw had saved him from more misery than he could remember—from spewing in the heat of the moment that he loved a girl to bypassing an angry outburst in an unindulgent courtroom.

His emotions were on lockdown.

By the time he was an adult, though, the problem was that the clamped mouth had become a bit of a giveaway—a *tell*, according to his first true mentor. Practicing law in a courtroom as a trial lawyer was a bit like playing poker...and you never wanted to give your emotions away. Be cool. Be calm. Not only did you want them to *never see you sweat,* you wanted to look a bit like a statue. Everything you did on the courtroom floor was for show—and your audience was watching and judging every moment. So Brock then had to learn how to clench his jaw only in the figurative sense. Unless he was emoting for the sake of the jury's attention, his facial expression wouldn't waver from looking studious, thoughtful, and serious.

In the boardroom with his father and two older brothers, though, it was a bit harder. Under that kind of stress, his emotions often took a trip down memory lane, and he had to make a conscious effort to keep his face neutral.

Today the stakes were high. "Thank you all for coming," said his father in his deep voice that still sometimes shook him to the core. And what was with the "you all," like it was a staff meeting or something? Like Brock had seen since the first time he'd attended a meeting that his father led, the older man's hands, still strong but covered in looser skin, were folded in front of him on the table, precise and ready to strike. His posture was perfect, making him look tall even while seated. And at 65, women found Brady Ford attractive, even with the white hair and gray goatee, making Brock believe it was due to his formidable presence. "My sons, you have made me proud. Each one of you is a fine attorney and you would be a wonderful addition to any team, but I've been fortunate: Not only did my sons want to follow in my footsteps but they wanted to work for me. How many fathers have had that pleasure?"

Brock would have loved to correct his father. Maybe his brothers were different, but Brock had never gathered that he'd had any choice in the matter. That said, he'd always felt like he had something to prove, so rather than specializing in business law (like his oldest brother Bret) or property law (like their middle brother Brandon), Brock had chosen criminal law. What his brothers had chosen ensured that the money would continue to flow like a waterfall through Ford & Associates. Brock's area of expertise merely ensured that he would continue to be the black sheep and the only thing that saved him was that he toyed with the occasional tort to rake in the dough.

But he was a lawyer, dammit…and a good one.

"I didn't ask you here to praise you, though. I think the three of you know that I've reached a point in my life where I'm ready to

2

hand over the reins to you, and you have all proven yourselves worthy. The details haven't been worked out yet, but there's time for that. In the meantime, your mother is planning a large event to make the announcement. There will be dinner and possibly press. I expect you all to be there."

"When will it be?" Of course, Bret would be the one to ask, always sucking up to their father. Between that and the fact that he looked like their mother with his blond hair, green eyes, and olive skin, it was no wonder he was their father's favorite.

"Wednesday evening at seven."

Brock felt his jaw growing tight again. Something this big, this important, shouldn't have been sprung on them last minute. It was inconsiderate and rude—but it was also quite typical of his father. As always, he was expected to be the center of their universe.

And he also liked to keep his sons on their toes.

When he asked, "Any other questions?" Brock knew it was best to keep his mouth shut. His father had a habit of expecting questions to be asked *before* the end of the meeting—in context, when questions were relevant. It was only a polite gesture that he asked at the end, and that was thanks to dealing with thoughtful clients over the years. But it was clear that this meeting was over.

So Brock moved his head just enough that it was clear he had nothing to ask. He stood, buttoning his black jacket, and nodded to his father and brothers before walking toward the door. It wasn't the first time that it struck him just how different he was from the other men in his family. Bret looked like their mother; Brandon looked like their father had at his age—brown hair with eyes to match; but Brock even *looked* the black sheep with his dark brown hair and blue eyes. What made him striking was the dimples he'd fought so hard to hide. Had he not had an uncle with the same features, he might have thought he'd been the product of an affair, and who could have blamed his mother? His father was gone from home a lot when Brock had been younger, and even when his body had been in the house, his mind was on his law firm and often his eyes were in a brief he'd brought home to "peruse" after dinner.

Whatever would the man do with his time now?

It wasn't Brock's problem. When he'd left for college, he'd never returned home—to live anyway. He'd come home in the figurative sense, taking a position in the firm as expected, but he'd never moved back in his parents' house. He relished his freedom more than anything else, and his ties to the firm were his only chains.

Trying to hustle down the hall so he could do some strategizing—because he now knew what he had to do to ensure equal footing with his brothers in the firm when his father handed control to them—he fell short. It was only seconds before Brandon caught up with him.

Brandon with his baby face, the one who could have been mistaken for their dad in days gone by, was the least confident of all the brothers. A stranger never would have been able to tell, but the way Brandon questioned everything left no doubt in Brock's mind. "Wait up, Brock." He paused and turned slightly, still fighting the urge to grind his teeth. Brandon's voice was low as he began walking with Brock down the hall. "We all know dad's retiring, but do you know what the big deal is? Why is he going to announce it publicly next week?"

"Because dad likes to do stuff for show, Brandon. This is free publicity for the firm if he invites the right people—and it's like passing the torch. Sure, we've been here for a while, but dad still has his own personal clients who probably don't trust us. It's his way of ensuring them that everything will be okay even after he's left."

Brock was *not* going to tell Brandon his other theory.

"Yeah?"

"What else could it be?"

Brandon shrugged. "So you don't think I need to worry about anything coming out of left field?"

No, but Brock did—and that was why he needed some time alone. "What've you got to worry about, Bran? You've never had clients complain to dad about you and you don't screw stuff up. Relax."

Brock tried to get away but Brandon grabbed his arm by the elbow. "You don't think dad's giving control of the firm to Bret, do you?"

Yes, he'd thought of that—Bret was the pet, after all—but he didn't think that was going to happen. "Anything's possible, Bran. You know that. And if he does, then what? You still have a job, right? You're still a partner. So what if he has ultimate control?"

4

His brother pursed his lips but then said, "I guess you're right."

"The bottom line—if dad's already made up his mind, you can't do much to change it now." Even though that was *exactly* what Brock planned to do. "Go home and have a stiff drink. Spend some time with Lisa and the baby. Don't think about this place till tomorrow."

"Good advice. I think I'll take you up on it."

Brock let out a slow breath. He had to think fast, without his brother distracting the shit out of him, because he knew exactly what his father would do—and there was no sense letting Brandon know, because it wouldn't affect him negatively. When Brock had first joined the firm five years earlier (after working as a clerk every summer since his junior year in college), his father had sat all three sons down and told them he was planning to retire in the next ten years and that he wanted his firm run by family men. Brock's ears had perked up at that. He'd barely started living; he'd hardly tasted his freedom. The last thing he'd wanted to do was settle down like Bret and Brandon, being ratcheted down by wives and children and housing costs. No way. He planned to enjoy life as a bachelor for as long as possible.

But his father believed that married men made for more reliable businessmen, lawyers, and partners. They had a vested interest to continue working and working hard. They had a reason to get up in the morning, because they had people counting on them. Brady Ford had never said it out loud, but his youngest son had heard it loud and clear: *If you want to inherit my firm someday, I expect you to have a family.*

It didn't matter that Brock was the youngest nor that he was a damn good lawyer without the fetters.

His father always got his way, and if he didn't, punishment followed. What that meant to Brock was that, if he wasn't a family man, he wouldn't be a full managing partner in the firm. He could be fired at the whim of his brothers if they both chose to do it—and, with his maverick style of courtroom antics, he could see one or both of his siblings deciding to give him a boot.

It was time to take matters into his own hands.

It was time to control his destiny.

Brock Ford was on a mission.

*   *   *

Erica Larson ran her fingers through her light brown hair before letting out a long breath. She stared at the pile of files on the table and shook her head before standing up. She needed another cup of coffee if she was going to get through all this crap before eight o'clock.

This was not what she'd imagined for herself when she'd enrolled in pre-law classes at the University of Denver, and this was most certainly not what she'd envisioned when she'd then been accepted into their law school. She'd wanted to fight for justice for the little guy or help put a bad guy behind bars—she hadn't expected to be drowning in research.

Endless research.

Instead of feeling like an attorney, she felt like an archaeologist as each discovery led to something else. It was like digging up a dinosaur, and not until you had located all the bones did you know your job was complete.

It was utterly unsatisfying.

Over the past week, she'd been contemplating moving back home to Gunnison on the western slope of Colorado. Surely, she could find law work there or even hang her own shingle—*local girl makes good*. That alone would probably help her start her own business, even without much experience. And her mom and dad still maintained her old bedroom and had told her their door was always open.

But she was determined to make it. She just didn't know that Ford & Associates was the right place to do it. After accepting their offer of employment a year ago (after clerking with them for quite a while before that), she'd known she'd have to do a little grunt work to prove herself. This was ridiculous, though. She was doing paralegal work and growing damn sick and tired of it.

For now, though…*coffee.* She needed caffeine to help her think clearly. She could wait till Sunday to contemplate her future. And she fully intended to. This weekend, she was going to outline exactly what she'd say to Bret Ford, her boss, and then give him an ultimatum on Monday morning: either she start doing more significant work, or she was gone. And then she had to be prepared to be shown the door. At this point, she knew that was fine. Better to live free, happy, and poor than be buried under a mountain of mind-numbing bullshit paperwork, financially comfortable but not living life.

She made her way to the break room still feeling foggy. Although she could neither see nor hear other people in the building, she knew they were there. Like herself, there were about a dozen or so newbies who felt like they had to bust their asses to keep up with the work and either get noticed or risk unemployment. So it surprised her when she saw that not only was the coffee pot empty, it had been turned off. Crazy people.

Erica held the carafe under the faucet, trying to decide if she wanted to make a full or half pot. As she was pouring the water into the machine, she heard footsteps. It was probably Mankin, the guy from the second floor who'd been working past six the last three weeks. He'd tried hitting on her once or twice but Erica wasn't interested. She'd told him there was no time for romance with the kind of hours she put in, but it was really that she felt no chemistry with the guy. In fact, she was pretty sure she would feel more sparks with a piece of whole wheat toast.

But the man who'd entered the room *wasn't* Mankin. If she was correct, he was the youngest Ford brother.

Bret had hired her, had taken her around the first floor to introduce her to some of her coworkers, but had never bothered to show her the rest of the building, nor let her meet the rest of his family who ran the firm.

Shit. She should have studied up on them, because now she was going to look like an uncaring jerk and who knew how much that could hurt her future here at the firm. Then again, maybe that would be the push she would need to leave. It might be a good thing.

So she decided to play dumb—even though the way this guy looked made her feel dumfounded. He was freaking gorgeous from head to toe—dark hair slicked back, striking bone structure that somehow made him look all business, with eyes the color of a cool pool of water. She could easily get lost in those eyes. And he wasn't the tallest guy she'd ever met, but his presence somehow made him feel like he was towering over her.

Then she knew—this had to be the youngest brother, the trial lawyer, the one who walked fearlessly into a courtroom, in spite of the fact that his older brothers had never seen one. Of course, that was all gossip, but feeling how his entire being took up the whole room, she wouldn't have doubted it for a second.

The grapevine had never mentioned just how captivating he was, though. He was taking her breath away.

She swallowed and dumped the scoops of coffee into the basket, keeping her hands busy since her brain was buzzing.

"Mind if I have a cup when it's done?"

She had to force her tongue to work, but there was no helping the nervous crack in her voice. "No, not at all." Then she felt a little surge of irritation. After all, this guy was a brother of the man who was keeping her buried in a cave piled high with paperwork. They were all cut from the same cloth—so she needed to set him straight right this second. "Me first."

His lips turned up ever so slightly, as if he found her amusing. Oh, shit. He had dimples. That made him look even more appealing. *Wolf in sheep's clothing.* "Of course." His simple response pissed her off more, as if he knew he was getting under her skin, but she wasn't going to say another word. No sense giving him fuel for the fire.

Damn. Was this the world's slowest coffee pot or what? And why the hell had she chosen to make a full pot?

"How long have you been here?"

Still feeling like a rabbit in headlights, she wondered why he cared. "Just a few minutes. Right before you got here."

Then he chuckled, the sounds of it mocking her. "No. I mean with Ford & Associates."

Her eyes connected with his again, and that was when she felt the full intensity of his gaze. Holy shit. Was he checking her out or scrutinizing her as a permanent employee? And she knew she looked like crap—midway in the day, she'd pulled her hair into a loose bun held in place with a pencil. Sure, she was wearing makeup, never leaving home without it, and her business suit ensured that she looked like she belonged there, but she was certain she appeared frazzled and tired—both of which were true. The coffee would help her *feel* better but it certainly wouldn't help the way she looked.

Why the hell was she trying to impress this guy?

Swallowing the pool of saliva that had filled her mouth, she answered, "Officially or otherwise?"

He chuckled again, this would-be mysterious stranger. "Both."

8

"I've been employed as an attorney of law for about a year, but I've been working here for two."

"Why haven't I seen you here before?"

She wanted to tell him it was because he was stuck in his ivory tower on the third floor. "I've been doing nothing but research since I got here. I've been stuck in a conference room for months with files and a computer and not much else." Continuing to play dumb, she said, "What about you?" He raised his eyebrows. "How long have *you* been here?"

His smile was smug—half a turn on and half making her stomach turn. "Five years or so. But you could say I've been studying the business for decades."

Ah...so *now* he was going to reveal who he was. She couldn't continue to play dumb—but if he thought she was going to bow down to him, he was sadly mistaken. Instead, at the last second, she decided to employ a little humor—all while wishing the damn coffee would finish brewing already. "You look good for your age. Decades, huh? You must be at least fifty then."

The handsome man then burst into laughter—and the dimples in his cheeks were impossible to miss at that point. God...she was in trouble. This man was captivating and, in spite of everything in her that told him he was nothing but bad news, she was drawn to him like a magnet. He stuck out his hand then, all business. "I'm Brock Ford." She extended her arm to shake but she again lost her tongue. As her smaller hand slid into his strong warm one, she felt as though a bolt of electricity passed through her entire body. What would that hand feel like in other places?

Stop. If she didn't get herself under control, she was bound to make a fool of herself. Fortunately, she'd practiced talking to a judge and jury even though she'd never done it, but she tried to get her head in that space before she answered. "Erica Larson."

"So you're not enjoying what my brother has you doing?"

Oh, shit. Had she said too much and jeopardized her job? Well...as she'd thought earlier, maybe it would be better that way. Honesty was the best policy. "Let's just say it's not what I signed up for—but I realize I have to pay my dues." The question was if she was willing to stick around that long while the firm ate her soul alive.

"I think I might have a proposition for you...if you wouldn't mind drinking your coffee in my office."

On the third floor?

Proposition?

"Do you have five minutes?"

Knowing this might all be a test about loyalty or general state of mind, she hesitated and then told him the truth. "Not really. I need to finish all the shit scattered on my table, go home, sleep for five hours, shower, and come back and do it again."

His response was golden. No raised eyebrows at the expletive and she was certain she saw a smile lurking underneath his cool façade. "You can leave it till tomorrow. And if my brother gives you any grief about it, you can send him to me."

With his permission to leave her work behind, Erica wouldn't have been able to stop herself any more than a dam with a giant crack could stop the flow of water. But she couldn't let him know how eager she was to follow him, just in case he was the Pied Piper and not Jesus Christ. Instead, she said, "I'm intrigued," and again wished the coffee would hurry the hell up…but this time, for completely different reasons.

CHAPTER TWO

SO FAR, THIS had been entirely too easy. Most things Brock Ford wanted involved hard work and determination. But this had been simple. He'd made up his mind earlier this afternoon exactly what he planned to do and he'd lucked out. The first woman he'd spied before leaving for the evening had been the perfect candidate for his scheme—she was well dressed, beautiful, and, he had to assume, smart.

Now he only had to convince her—and, with his track record in the courtroom, that shouldn't be too difficult.

His office, a place where he negotiated plea agreements and convinced clients to take what was offered, was the perfect location for him to strike a deal with this lovely creature.

Erica Larson was his type—and he knew if he was going to have his family believe this scheme, the woman had to be the kind of female he'd fall for. She was tall and thin but not overly so. She had lovely breasts hidden under typical lawyer attire—blouse and jacket over a pencil skirt. And those legs were just as lovely as the rest of her. What captivated him the most, though, were her brown eyes. They seemed to match her light brown hair, pulled up onto her head in a careless but endearing manner.

If he wasn't careful, he was going to fall for the ruse he was about to present to his family.

But, first, he had to convince Ms. Larson that his plan would help her, too.

After they sat, she sipped her coffee, the look on her face part pensive, part irritated—no doubt because he'd torn her away from her evening's work and she was hoping to get home before the Late Show. "As I said downstairs, Erica..." He paused, then asked, "Do you mind if I call you Erica?"

"No. That's my name."

The way she arched her eyebrow was cute as hell. He was going to enjoy working with this girl. "I have a bit of a proposition for you. I'm going to tell you right now that's it's highly unorthodox."

A slight smile crept upon her face. A fellow rebel, perhaps? That would be good because she'd need to be an ally to follow through. He hadn't quite figured out his argument yet but it was going to revolve around her, so let the interrogatories begin.

"How do you feel thus far about your employment with Ford & Associates?" The quickness with which she inhaled and started to form an answer told him she was getting ready to pour out a mouthful of bullshit—and *that* he did not need. "I want an honest answer." He leaned over the desk a bit, his hands folded in front of him. "And, Ms. Larson, bear in mind I'm a criminal attorney. I will know if you're lying." He was using his courtroom voice, the one he questioned unreliable witnesses with. He knew it could be intimidating, and that was exactly what he wanted to do with this young lady if she was considering fibbing.

She raised her eyebrows and cleared her throat. "What happened to calling me Erica?"

He allowed a slight smirk to form on his lips. "I'll only be friendly if you're telling me the truth."

She nodded, acting like something might be caught in her throat, but then she spoke. "Well, I think I probably already let the cat out of the bag. What I've been doing the past year? It's not what I went to law school for. I get that I need to pay my dues, but..."

Perfect. "You can call me Brock, by the way. And how would you feel if I told you I could get you out of file slavery and doing what you *really* want to do?"

Erica tilted her head slightly, causing a shiny lock of hair to tumble out of her makeshift bun. "I'd ask what price that privilege came with."

"Ah, you are a smart woman. And, yes, there is a price, but I can assure you it's probably not what you'd expect. It should be fairly simple, and I can have you working upstairs with me in less than a week."

The twinkle in her eyes was all he needed to see to know he'd struck the nerve he wanted to. He'd caught the fish; now all he had to do was reel her in. "I'm listening."

"For what I'm about to tell you, I should have you sign a nondisclosure agreement…so, suffice it to say, this is confidential."

"Of course."

Something in him told him he could trust her, so he was going to move forward. If she turned him down and went to one of his brothers with her story, he could laugh it off—but he hoped she'd actually agree. "My father is getting ready to retire. Since I first entered law school, just like my two older brothers, dad began promising the firm to us when he was ready to stop practicing. But by the time I actually *joined* the firm, he'd added a caveat to his earlier promise." He continued assessing her interest by watching her eyes—and so far, so good. "I'd been here about a year when he took Bret, Brandon, and me to Lake Tahoe one weekend as a getaway. I thought it was just to celebrate the fact that the Ford men were all in business together, but there was more to it. Dad let us know the kind of partners he wanted us to be—honest, reliable, hardworking men of integrity."

Erica nodded. "I'd think any lawyer with those qualities would make a good partner."

Brock smiled. "Yes. But dad also said flat out that he expected all three of us to get married and have families—he all but said, 'I won't make you partner if you don't.' I got a little angry then. You know as well as I do that it's hard to have a relationship when you're married to your work."

Her voice was cool but he thought he could hear irritation in her voice. "I don't see you or your brothers working late every night."

"I did when I first started here—I clocked around seventy or eighty hours a week at the office. But, unlike other law firms, that's not what my father values. He believes that a good attorney has a loving family behind him." Erica raised her eyebrows, signaling that she maybe thought it was as ridiculous a notion as he did. "He also thinks it keeps them on the straight and narrow path—you're less likely to do something shady when you have people at home relying on you to keep yourself out of trouble.

"Old fashioned, I know.

"But that's my dilemma, Erica. I'm not ready for marriage." He was *not* going to spend the next five minutes divulging the entire truth, that not only was he not interested in a wife, but he was nowhere near ready to settle down, even with "just" a girlfriend. He might not have been married to the job as he implied he'd been when he first began his career, but he loved the idea of having a different woman whenever he chose. In fact, there were two different attorneys he played around with on occasion—one was with the DA's office—who were about as close to a regular lay as they came, but even they couldn't lay claim to his heart. "When dad gave us this ultimatum, for lack of a better word, Brandon was the only one of us three who was even married. I think that was all Bret needed to hear to marry his girlfriend, and Brandon and Lisa started talking about having kids within two years of that speech. I figured, *eh, I got time*.

"But the years crept up on me—and dad said earlier today that he'll be formally announcing his retirement next week. I hadn't expected it so soon. And when dad was telling us about it, he didn't mention the whole you-have-to-be-a-family-man-to-inherit-the-business thing, but it was unspoken. And he's going to announce his retirement publicly, too. Here's the thing—I could see dad telling Bret and Brandon that, once I married, he'd want them to cut me in, but once dad's no longer in control, he won't be able to guide their decisions. Yes, we're technically partners now but in name only. Dad calls all the shots. When he retires, he'll actually be giving us control of the firm—and he won't give that to me if I don't have a family."

Brock couldn't read Erica's face. Was she amused? Annoyed? Disgusted? A little weirded out by it all? "If you think I'm going to run to the Justice of the Peace with you tonight, you're out of your mind. I realize it's easy enough to annul that kind of thing, but I don't want a headache like that."

"No, I don't want anything that extreme, either. I need a woman—someone believable—to attend dad's dinner with me next week, posing as my fiancée. If I thought getting married today would solve the problem, don't think I wouldn't—but my family wouldn't buy it for one second. A recent and secret engagement? They might buy that—and that's what I'm banking on: that they will."

Erica was quiet for a moment, looking down at her hands on the table. In that instant, Brock felt a tiny bit of affection for her, because she already acted the part of seasoned lawyer—she was absorbing the proposition, weighing her options, possibly deciding on a counteroffer or thinking of terms to suggest. "So you want *me* to pretend I'm engaged to you?"

"That's the gist of it, yes."

"How would that work exactly?"

"Well, you'd show up with me to dad's little soiree. I'd introduce you to everyone and tell them we had a whirlwind romance, that we've fallen madly in love and want to get married next spring—or something like that. And then, once all the ink has dried on the paperwork that puts my brothers and me on equal footing, you and I 'break up,' saying it just wasn't working out."

Erica was quiet again, once more contemplating, and he wanted to give her the time to do it. As much as he would have loved to tell her to just make up her mind, he suspected she needed a few minutes to wrap her mind around it, try it on for a good fit.

She really was the perfect woman for it—her looks were right and the fact that she was an attorney, unlike her brothers' spouses, would make this scenario all the more believable. Or so he thought.

"That's it? I just show up to this party pretending to be your fiancée?"

"You'll probably have to put on a show for a little longer. Until dad actually retires and hands it over to us…"

Erica nodded but was silent for a few more moments. "And what's in it for me?"

"Like I said, I'll get off the back room on the first floor and actually practicing law." Her eyes searched his as he added, "That's what you want, isn't it?"

"Yes…but I also know I have to earn it."

She wasn't going to make this easy. "Look…are you a good attorney?"

"I'd like to think so."

"Then don't you think you should be practicing law—instead of slaving away doing endless hours of research?" He lowered his voice as if sharing a secret. "Isn't that what we pay paralegals to do?"

"Yes." Brock could see doubt in her eyes and she finally spat it out. "But what guarantee do I have that, once we 'break up,' I'm not forced back into my little hole?" Or how can I even trust that you'll keep me here at the firm? How do I know you won't fire me when all's said and done?"

Shit. She had a point there—and she had very good reason to be paranoid. But she didn't know Brock. In spite of the fact that he was a mad dog in the courtroom—vicious and heartless—his dad had instilled a sense of integrity in him and his brothers, a need to be honest. Of course, the fact that he was putting on a huge show to deceive them all sort of negated that—so why should she believe him? She was viewing duplicity from him from the get go. Why should she think anything different?

He shrugged, not knowing what to say. There would be no "you just gotta trust me," because she didn't know him from Adam. There was no reason why she *should* find him trustworthy.

"I guess you don't." He cocked an eyebrow. "But you yourself said you don't like what you're doing. If I get you up here, working cases with me and—"

"Hold on. That's part of the problem. I can't be working cases *with* you. If I'm working with you and we are no longer a couple, why would you keep working with me? That doesn't make sense."

"We were friends before."

"Would your family really believe that?"

She was quick. He loved that. Being on her toes like this meant she'd be able to play the role of his fiancée easily—and that made him all the more determined to convince her. "Okay. We'll get you your own office and cases. I'll work with you for a little bit until we feel like you've got it, and then I'll back off. That way, when we break up, you're already established and no one thinks twice about it."

"I don't know..." He allowed her to think through her pause. "Brock." But that gap in her words was instead her way of allowing herself to say his name for the first time.

He shouldn't have enjoyed the way her lips and mouth wrapped around those syllables as much as he did. It was a reminder that this woman was most definitely his type, and he started imagining her as another gazelle ripe for the takedown—but he couldn't. She was going to be his partner in crime, so to speak, so he had to keep his hands off for fear of ruining the deal.

"Would *you* want to spend a lot of time around, say, your ex-girlfriends?"

Brock wasn't a huge fan. They were nice enough women but she was right. He wouldn't want to be anywhere near them, no matter how well (or not) he felt like he knew them. "Should we draw up a contract? Make it seem like a prenup but instead make it agreeable to both parties?"

Erica arched her lovely eyebrow again but a small smile formed in her corner of her mouth. "We write it together? And we sign it *before* you make your big announcement?"

Was she saying yes? He sat up, poker face intact. "I think that's agreeable. Do we have a deal?"

She stuck out her hand and Brock took it in his. It was lovely—smooth and warm, and he could feel the delicate bones, in spite of the fact that she had a strong handshake...just as a lawyer should, especially a female with something to prove. "Deal."

11:32. That was what the green LED light on her bedtime clock said.

Erica rolled over in bed, struggling to sleep—and that was stupid. She was beyond tired. But she'd gotten home a lot earlier than she had in months and, excited, she tackled a few projects she'd been avoiding, things like thinning out the unwanted clothes in her closet, washing the inside of the fridge, and the like—but her mind had been on Brock the whole time.

He'd offered to draw up the initial fake prenuptial agreement. There would be the standard financial and asset items found in all prenups, but he'd add more about her professional career not being screwed with, no matter the outcome of their "marriage." They both agreed that, even though they wouldn't follow through with matrimony, the intent was there, and if she didn't keep her job, she'd be able to plead with a judge that it all counted from the moment of signing. Brock swore he'd be an upstanding guy—and there was no reason not to be. She was doing him a huge favor. If he ousted her, what would stop her from blowing his cover?

Nothing.

Her biggest fear was what his brothers would want to do. There was no guarantee that the middle brother Brandon would like her despite her role as Brock's love interest, and Bret might be upset that she was being pulled from research, but Erica knew already that she wouldn't want to go back to doing what she'd been doing. Not now. She was far too excited to begin acting like a real attorney rather than one in title only. There was nothing more she could learn from conducting research. She knew now that if she needed to find something, she wouldn't have to rely on a paralegal to do it for her, but that didn't mean she wanted to do research and nothing but research for the rest of her career. Life was far too short for that.

When they'd parted earlier that evening, Brock had asked her to stick it out with her old job until the announcement next Wednesday, but he added that his brother would have no idea if she hadn't been there all night—and did it really matter? The research files kept coming, no matter how many she finished. There was no end in sight. Why not leave that for someone who had a passion for it, like Charley, the clerk who'd been with the firm since its inception?

She was destined for bigger and better things.

Brock had told her they would spend the next week working through the fake prenup. He'd email it to her once he was done and let her look it over and make any changes necessary. Once they were happy, they'd sign it in front of his secretary, a woman who was also a notary public, and then the game was on.

It all seemed so simple.

Erica rolled over again. The damn clock mocked her. 11:34. And she was no closer to sleep than she'd been an hour ago when she lay down.

Sitting up, she flipped on the lamp on her bedside table. She couldn't remember the last time she'd struggled with drifting off. This job had left her so sleep deprived, her head would hit the pillow and she'd find herself in dreamland seconds later. Something was bothering her—aside from the fact that she was going to be playing make believe—and she needed to get to the root of it. Then, perhaps, she could sleep for a few hours before having to awaken.

She picked up the little book sitting behind the lamp. It had an ocean blue cover made of fabric, and there were no words on it, just a pattern of little red, green, and blue designs in the cloth. Cracking it open, she flipped through the thin lined pages. About halfway through, she saw that the last entry she'd made had been over a year ago, the night before her graduation.

Words. Just words. She'd been so eager, so excited, but even then, she'd had doubts. She'd already been clerking at Ford & Associates, and the writing had been on the wall. She'd predicted—*correctly*—that she wouldn't be actually practicing law for a while. Granted, she'd still had to pass her bar exam, but that wouldn't take forever. In fact, reading through her entry, she saw that she'd expected to be practicing actual law by January. And here it was November—almost a year after she'd expected to be in the thick of things—and the only reason she was even close now was because of this stupid bargain she was making.

She *was* going to do it, right?

Well...it wasn't like she was actually going to marry Brock. There was no denying the guy was hot—super hot. Part of the problem was that he knew it. His face was ridiculously handsome—gorgeous blue eyes and dark hair—and he seemed to have the body to match. Under his expensive, beautifully tailored suit, she had no way of knowing for certain, but she suspected he took good care of himself from head to toe.

Yeah, he was good looking, the kind of guy she'd gaze at across a crowded bar or down the street while waiting for the light to turn so she could safely walk to the other side—but once he opened his mouth, she'd lose all interest. It was clear from their short but productive conversation that Brock Ford hadn't entered law to do good things. Unlike herself, who'd entered law so she could defend the downtrodden, help good people find justice, and right wrongs, the youngest Ford seemed to have entered the family business because, one, his brothers had and it was expected, and, two, he was all about the money. Well, not just the cash but the prestige and fame. He was a hotshot.

No, he was a prick.

If he'd been the guy she'd seen at a bar and been intrigued by, as soon as he'd started talking, her lady boner would have gone limp. Yes, he was confident, hot, and sexy—and that would make pretending to be his fiancée easy. The problem would be when he opened his mouth.

So, like Brock, she hoped their engagement would be short lived—that, as he predicted, his father would hand over the firm to his sons right after Christmas (and maybe even before)...and the two of them could go their separate ways.

The irreconcilable differences part wouldn't be difficult to fake.

No…it was the next two months that would be hard.

But she'd be doing what she'd set out to do years ago when she'd taken her first prelaw class and knew this was her dream. She'd be acting like a *real* attorney. Rather, she wouldn't be *acting*; she'd be *doing*. And she wouldn't have to fake that shit at all.

She was writing furiously in her journal for the first time in ages, and sometime close to one, she'd closed her eyes to think about her last few thoughts but drifted off and didn't shut off the lamp until she felt the pen drop from her hand half an hour later.

And she dreamed about being a *real* attorney.

When she awoke, her mind was made up. She'd do whatever it took to get there—even play Brock Ford's bride to be. It would be a piece of cake.

CHAPTER THREE

DRESSED IN A soft pink t-shirt, faded blue jeans, and a light black coat, Erica stood next to the short line in Starbucks while looking out the window. She saw her best friend Camilla's car turn into the parking lot before the woman maneuvered into a parking space and got out of her car.

Oh, it had been too long, thanks to her stupid damn job. She and Camilla had become best friends when they'd both been sophomores at DU, but Camilla had been a business major, and she'd graduated with her MBA a couple of years before Erica finished law school. They used to get together for lunch once a week, but since Erica had become immersed in research hell at Ford & Associates and Camilla had found the love of her life, their weekly lunches had become monthly ones. They still texted and talked once in a while, but both women were emerged in their own worlds. In fact, the last time they'd done something together, Camilla was busy talking about all her wedding preparation, making Erica decide right then and there that she wanted nothing to do with a traditional wedding, if that time ever came. Nope, she'd rather elope to Vegas and be done with it. All that money and time for the perfect romantic wedding felt like major bullshit—too much money and preparation for an hour or two of torture when all the couple really wanted to do was declare their love for each other and spend the rest of their lives together.

Camilla walked in the door, pulling down the hood of her jacket, and her red hair tumbled out, looking messy but pretty.

During the week, her friend would pull her hair back into a bun or a ponytail but, away from the office, she'd let her hair go wild. She often looked to Erica like a lion, fierce and proud. As she got closer, Erica smiled and held out her arms to hug her friend.

"Hey, I'm glad you suggested this. You finally emerged from your cave! And the best part—traffic wasn't too bad this morning." Camilla's green eyes sparkled. "I can't wait to hear this big announcement."

Erica grinned, leading the way into the line proper. "Well, don't get *too* excited. It's not what you think—but I'm bursting at the seams. I have to tell *someone*." After they'd both ordered lattes and stood at the corner of the counter waiting to hear their names, Erica asked, "So how are the wedding plans coming?"

Camilla half frowned. "Oh, they're a pain in the ass. Mainly because Gary's an only child and his mother has huge plans. I don't know a nice way to tell her that my parents had offered to foot part of the bill, too, but I've turned them down because I know what I want. If it's *my* money, I should have the wedding I want. But Gary's mom is so worried about appearances…"

"Sorry."

"No. I need to learn to diplomatically deal with her, you know? This is going to be the first of many negotiations." When Erica started to laugh, Camilla said, "No, seriously. I don't need her telling me what schools to send my children to or what daycare center is best or why they shouldn't eat tofu." Erica nodded. She hadn't thought of that. Just another reason to not get serious with anyone. And that was just fine with her. Now she was going to finally be able to focus on her career—and that was more important than a relationship. "But what about you?"

The barista slid both their drinks out on the counter within seconds of each other, and the two women gravitated toward a table beside a window that looked out on the busy street. "Still working away."

"Yeah, but what about this outrageous news you keep teasing me about?"

Erica had been trying to decide how to tell her best friend how crazy her life was about to become—but, not knowing how Camilla would react had made her rethink what to say dozens of times. She only knew she had to tell someone—and Camilla was it. They'd kept each other's secrets like buried treasure for several years now. That wasn't about to change.

Sipping her hot venti mocha, Erica took in a slow breath through her nostrils. When she set her cup down on the table, she asked, "Did you ever play house with neighbor kids?"

"Well, yeah. Who didn't?"

Erica nodded, glad her friend was on board thus far. "I'm going to be doing the adult version of that, starting next week."

"The *adult version*? What does that even mean?"

"So…you know Ford & Associates is owned by Brady Ford and his sons are partners?"

"Um, maybe?" Camilla winced. "Sorry. I guess I don't pay much attention to the details of your job."

Erica let out a soft chuckle. "I think you have a little bit on your own plate." And she doubted she could return the favor of knowing many specifics about her friend's job, which made them even. "So there are three sons. The deal is that, when father Ford retires, he plans to pass the business on to his sons—but only if they are family men."

"Meaning?" Camilla had picked up her cup to take a sip but hadn't yet.

"Meaning they need to be married or well on the way. I guess Senior Ford feels like family guys are more reliable and work harder."

"Or *not*. Gary used to work seventy or eighty hours a week until we started dating hardcore. Now that we're living together, he works even less. And it doesn't really matter—he's on salary anyway. Sure, he works more from home than he ever did, and sometimes on Saturdays, I have to beg him to shut off the computer, but he's always home before seven on weeknights." She finally took a sip from her cup. "It wasn't always that way."

"Hey, I don't make up the rules. I'm just telling you what I heard the old guy thinks."

"But the *news*…"

"I'm getting there. So the oldest and middle brothers are married already. The middle brother even has a child and I think the oldest has one child on the way or maybe they're just thinking about it. I'm not sure. But the youngest one, Brock, is nowhere near even considering marriage. I think he's been having too much fun playing the field."

Camilla arched a perfectly trimmed eyebrow. "So where do

you come in? Are you wanting to tame the wild beast?"

Erica sucked on her upper lip as she tried to decide how to delicately tell her friend some of the weirdest news in her life. "Not exactly." She let out a slow breath and then explained to Camilla all the events that had transpired a couple of days earlier. Her eyes grew wide several times during the conversation and she couldn't help even giggling once or twice.

"So he wants you to play his fiancée?" Erica nodded, knowing it sounded stupid. "What makes him think his family will fall for it?"

"I don't know. All I *do* know is it's going to get me out of research and into a space where I can actually practice law, putting my talents to good use before I completely forget them."

"Will you have to sleep with him? Or spend the night at his place or anything like that?"

It was something Erica hadn't considered. But she didn't need to. "Umm...*no*. Just no. The guy's an egomaniac—he's a slimeball. He's all about money, prestige, fame. He's arrogant and cocky. *No, thank you.*"

A sly smile spread over Camilla's face. "You should see your face. Methinks you protest too much."

"Well...the guy *is* hot. Really hot. He's the epitome of tall, dark, and handsome." She got ready to begin describing his looks and then stopped herself. It was simple enough to say, "Think of a young version of Jon Hamm with slightly lighter hair."

"Yum. So what's the problem? Just tune him out and stare."

"That's pretty hard. He has this commanding presence. He's not the kind of guy you can ignore...which is good, I guess, considering his favorite place is in the courtroom."

"So how long do you have to do it?"

"Just till the business is turned over to him and his brothers. Then, sometime after that, we 'break up,' telling everyone it just isn't working out. Once Brock owns his share of the business, they won't take it away from him. Especially since the whole 'family man' thing is an *unspoken* agreement."

"They won't shove you back into the research department then, will they?"

That was something Erica hadn't thought much about—and they hadn't done their "prenup" agreement yet. "I'm counting on it, but nothing's set in stone yet. It's death in research for me—I just can't stomach it anymore. But I have about two months to prove myself. If I can prove to them I'm better practicing law than conducting research, they'd be fools not to keep me doing that."

"But *what if,* Erica?"

She'd go back to what she'd already been contemplating on Monday, faced with another week of research purgatory. "If I go back to research after all that, then I'm moving home—and maybe hanging out my own shingle."

"What? Seriously? You'd come back for my wedding, though, right?"

"Oh, of course. I wouldn't miss it for the world."

"Good. Because I want you to be my maid of honor."

Erica felt her face begin to beam. Even though she and her friend had been besties since college, she hadn't thought much about Camilla's wedding plans. It really *was* an honor to even be considered. "Oh, my God, Cam. Wow. Yes. Of course."

"Excellent! Now...let's talk about *your* wedding..."

"Let's *not.*" Erica took a big swig of her coffee before she added, "If his mouth was closed, it would be easy. He really is a gorgeous guy. Pretending to be engaged to him would be simple because he's hot...but it's really not, because he's...*ugh.*"

"Is he really that bad?"

"Yes. And I suppose part of his behavior is founded. I mean he really does have the reputation of being all that in a courtroom. I just hate the smugness of it all."

"But if you don't have to kiss him or sleep with him or anything, but you get all the perks, what's the problem?"

Erica looked out the window in slow contemplation. "Nothing, I guess. As long as I can do a good job acting the part, it should be okay." Camilla nodded and smiled. "But I need your help with something."

"Name it."

"First of all, you are sworn to secrecy. You can't say a word to anyone, not even Gary."

Camilla's emerald eyes flashed and crinkled in a smile. "Fine. I think I can do that."

"Seriously, Camilla. Our coffee today was for me to tell you I'm engaged to Brock Ford."

"*Fine.* Then I want to meet this guy you're suddenly head over heels with."

Erica couldn't help but chuckle. "Fair enough."

"So what next?"

"I need your help, girlfriend. I have this retirement party thing next week. Something semiformal. All I've been wearing the past year has been suits for work and jeans and t-shirts on the weekends. I have *nothing* to wear to something like this. *Nothing.*"

"Then we're shopping as soon as we finish our coffee. How much money do you have on your credit card?"

"The question's not how much I have but how much I'm willing to spend on this silly scheme."

"I'd say these are billable expenses. How much is Brock Ford willing to spend?"

Erica smiled. "Hmm. I can text him and find out."

"Buy first; text later. You can always threaten to wear a gray DU sweatshirt and holey jeans to the party."

Both women erupted into gales of laughter. Yes, Erica had needed this badly. Time with her bestie was better than therapy.

Goddamn. Brock had spent the last several days having serious doubts about the plan he had concocted, but he felt no regrets as he walked into the restaurant's large private dining room with Ms. Erica Larson's arm linked in his. Sure, she looked cute, even a little mysterious, in her day-to-day business attire, but she'd really cleaned up for this. She'd chosen something a little daring—an off-the-shoulder red cocktail dress with an asymmetrical skirt and matching four-inch heels that made her look like a model. Her hair was pulled up loosely with a few wisps of hair falling here and there. She looked breathtaking, professional...and fuckable.

In other words, she fit the part of a woman Brock Ford would consider marrying. After all, if *he* was convinced, his family would be as well.

He'd started to wonder after their long lunch together on Monday, where they hammered out a prenuptial agreement they could both happy with. Most of it was standard—the property they owned before marriage would remain their own, yadda yadda yadda, but this unconventional pretend couple had more than that to worry about. He'd promised Erica to protect her position in the firm.

Not just the position she already held…but the one he was going to get her promoted to.

They had to take caution with the wording so it would look like they were talking about the position she held now but so that it would apply to any future positions she might hold in the firm. Of course, even that was easy enough to do, because, of course, anyone with a mind to practice law would want to move up the ladder.

Just that short time playing lawyer with her helped him realize she was a sharp cookie. She knew her stuff and, even though family law wasn't going to be her emphasis, she understood the ins and outs.

The perfect touch was when Harriet, his personal secretary, notarized the agreement. She took a shine to Erica, and that didn't happen too often. It had taken her over a year to be comfortable with Brock, not that he gave two shits. Now they understood each other and he wouldn't have another assistant if he could hand pick one. The woman was professional and understood him—but he suspected she hadn't liked him much when she'd first begun working for him.

Hell, she might not like him *now*.

But Brock focused on the present. He had the lovely Erica Larson on his arm and he had a couple of tricks up his sleeve. He was feeling confident about his plan and eager to move forward. As they entered the long dining room with her on his arm, he could tell by the looks several people gave him as they shared cursory greetings as he and Erica passed by, she was definitely convincing.

Well…as a *date*. He hadn't broken the engagement news yet.

Part of him felt bad that he was going to do it tonight—almost like trying to trump his father's news. But he knew that wasn't something to worry about. Everyone already knew dad was retiring, thus, the point of the playing the part in the first place. Tonight was all about details and pomp and circumstance. And *that*—hearing about future plans—was why Brock had Erica along. If his father already had hazy plans that were readying themselves to be set in concrete, he needed to let the old man know things in *his* life had changed.

The place where they were having this little party was in the heart of downtown Denver. Brock had never been to this particular place before, but it was intimate without being crowded.

27

It had an urban sense to it even while feeling upscale. At a glance, Brock was certain his parents had easily dropped a small fortune on the evening.

Yes, this was a huge deal.

As they walked farther in, he was even more impressed. This wasn't just a little get together. There had to be around two hundred people there. So much for intimate. They checked their coats and then he spied a server with a tray of champagne flutes. He'd been feeling a little nervous, but that was nothing compared to Erica's emotions. He could sense how uptight she was feeling. They could both use a little liquid relaxation. Taking two glasses, he handed her one. "Relax."

"Easy for you to say. I don't know anyone here."

"You know *me*. Oh, and Bret's around here somewhere. So that's two people you know. Technically, you know Brandon and my dad, too. So *four*. Four people." She gave him a look that was just short of an eye roll, meant to express disdain and irritation.

"I'm feeling a little on edge myself. I think anyone my dad ever called a close friend is here—I see old clients, other attorneys, both rivals and friends, judges, businessmen, politicians. There's practically a Who's Who of Denver here tonight." Brock took a large gulp of the champagne and then got close to Erica. The intent was to whisper in her ear so she would be the only one to hear him, but it had been a bad idea. Up close, he could smell the fragrance she wore. It was spicy, almost like cinnamon, and he would have loved nothing more at that moment than to bite her neck—or lick his tongue down her skin. As with most everything in his life, though, he was able to keep himself under control. "And this is the night I chose to begin the big lie. So at least you know we're in this together, darlin'."

Darlin'? Where the hell had *that* come from?

She might have been annoyed with him, but at least she believed the champagne was a good idea as well. He could tell because she was downing it faster than he was. "Come on," he said, linking her arm in his again so he could lead her all the way inside.

In spite of the fact that there were a lot of people talking, he could hear music overhead—piano was the main instrument but there were others involved. It was some classical piece but there would be no figuring out what is was over the low roar in the room. He spied a long table across the room where his mother was standing, but she was talking to a member of the wait staff. Brock had no idea where his father or brothers were, but both sisters-in-law already sat next to each other at the table where his mother was.

"We're headed over there." His intent was to avoid as many extra people as possible, because he knew most of the folks here. He wanted his parents to hear the story first. Bret walked over and said, "Glad you could make it. Dinner's served in five minutes."

"Just in time."

His oldest brother cocked his head, just the same way their mother did when she couldn't understand something. "You know Erica?"

A smirk formed on Brock's face. Wait'll he heard the big lie later on. "Yes, I think that's obvious. At least I don't need to introduce the two of you."

Bret got closer. "Go ahead and sit down. Mom's wanting to get started but she was waiting for you to get here."

Brock, biting his tongue, nodded and led the way once more. All the guests, as if sensing his mother's wishes, seemed to be heading toward their tables to sit down. It made it a little harder to get to the family table since there were lots of bodies in motion, but they would make it.

"Brock. How are you?"

"Doing great." He nodded at a man in dark gray suit. Then he leaned his head toward Erica while still moving forward. "That's Jensen Smithers. A decent attorney but a bit of an asshole. You'll get to know most of these guys soon enough."

"I haven't heard of him."

"He's not flashy. Doesn't do courtrooms much."

By the time they arrived at the table, Brandon was already seated next to Lisa. Fortunately, his parents had been wise enough to know Brock would bring a date. The surprise would come later. For now, he'd let them relish how gorgeous she was. The red dress really brought color to her face, making her cheeks look pink. Just lovely.

He noticed that they would have to sit on the other side of the table, next to his mother. Of course, she'd done everything in an unconventional way. It looked like dad would be seated at the head of the table, but his mother was at a diagonal from him. On the other side of dad was probably Bret (big surprise—but Brock wouldn't know for certain until his brother got to the table), followed by Elle, his wife, and Brandon's wife Lisa. Brock analyzed every possible place he could sit and decided that if he was playing a guy in love enough to want to marry, he'd want to be right next to his fiancée. Moving his lips to her ear again, he asked, "Would you rather sit beside my mother or brother?"

Erica inhaled deeply and he wanted to tell her to guzzle what was left in her flute. "Your brother."

He wasn't going to ask why, but it was likely because Erica had met Brandon once or twice. Or maybe mothers were more intimidating—but he had no idea why she'd made that choice. He waited until she sat to push her chair in and then he pulled out his own chair. His mother's eyes had been darting all over the room but she paused when she saw her son. "Brock, good to see you, son." She leaned toward him and kissed him on the cheek. As she pulled away, she asked, "Who's your date?"

"She works at the firm. I'll do introductions once we're seated."

Ah...mom didn't like that much, but she didn't have a choice. He sat just as his father and Bret joined the table. One of the servers approached his father and handed him a microphone. He said a few quick words into it, thanking everyone for coming, and then the crowd grew quiet and the last stragglers made their way to tables. "We're going to have dinner and then I want to speak to all of you for a bit. But, first, enjoy the meal." As he turned to the table before sitting down, he said, "I'm so glad all of you could make it. This would be nothing without my family here."

Dad hadn't said anything or even looked at Erica, but Brock knew his father had seen her. The first part was done. Now maybe he could truly loosen up a bit and try to eat.

They were well into the main course of beef medallions in bordelaise sauce surrounded by various vegetables, and Brock could tell Erica was a bit out of her element. He'd grown up eating meals like these where presentation was far more important than the actual meal, but Erica seemed to be pushing her food around more than she was eating it.

Then again, she was pretty thin—maybe that was why.

Brock's father had eaten most of the dinner on his plate and set his fork down. "So, Brock, why don't you introduce us to your date?"

Guess he'd have to be done eating, too. Placing his utensils on his plate, he said, "Everyone, this is Erica Larson. She works under Bret. Erica, this is my mother, Harper, and you know my father, Brady. I know you also know my brothers. But this," he said, indicating the woman directly across from himself, "is Elle, Bret's wife, and next to her is Lisa, Brandon's."

A shy smile covered Erica's face. He felt so grateful that she looked the part—she seemed graceful, beautiful, captivating, and he was sure his family would fall in love with her.

Brock's father looked at Erica, his face bathed in gentle smile, much like he often looked when he met a new employee. "So nice to meet you, Erica. I must apologize for not already meeting you. What's your specialty?"

"For the moment, it's research. But I'd actually love to get my feet wet in social justice and civil rights."

"Oh, are you an activist of sorts?"

"No, not really, but I got into law because I wanted to help people."

"Wonderful. That's a noble reason to join the ranks. But you're doing research now?"

Bret let out an embarrassed chuckle. "I've got her helping me with a couple of big tort cases right now, dad. We'll get her up and running soon."

"Actually," said Brock, "I was going to talk to you all about that. But, first, I have a bit of an announcement." He could see the shimmer in his mother's eyes. It was hope—the hope she'd had for all her children at different ages, usually having to do with milestones: graduation, marriage, babies. God, he almost felt like a complete dick pulling the wool over her eyes like this.

Almost.

He waited until his entire family's eyes were looking at him rather than their plates. "Erica and I met each other a while ago— she works some late evenings. We got to talking and, before you know it, we hit it off." Clearing his throat, he made sure everyone suspected what he was going to say before he spoke. "I know now that Erica is the love of my life. She is beautiful in every way

31

imaginable."

What followed were all the requisite gasps and giggles Brock had come to expect when delivering news like this and he wondered how his real engagement, possibly ten or twenty years in the future, would resemble this one. He could only hope that he was convincing enough. And he was pretty sure he had it in the bag, because what was coming next would even be a surprise to Erica, his pretend betrothed.

He could hardly wait.

CHAPTER FOUR

WOW. THIS WHOLE NIGHT thus far had been a little overwhelming. Erica had met a few rich kids in college, but in that environment, they'd been removed from their element, so they hadn't been too overbearing or obnoxious. She'd also encountered several wealthy attorneys now that she'd finished school, but nothing could have prepared her for the strange sensations she was feeling at the moment. Playing Brock's intended was pressure enough, along with trying to eat food designed to look like art rather than a meal. Being surrounded by obvious money really put a load on.

And the champagne hadn't helped.

Finally, in the middle of the main course, Brock decided it was time to break the news. He kept their supposed backstory simple but Erica wondered if telling everyone there that she was the "love of his life" was over the top. Would they question that statement when, a month or two later, they told everyone they couldn't stand each other?

Well, that was Brock's problem, not hers. Yes, she'd have to deal with it, too, but she could shift the blame to him fairly easily. He was domineering, overbearing, opinionated, arrogant…the list could go on and on as reasons why she couldn't picture herself married to him forever.

She wondered how long Brock was going to drag out his little speech, because everyone had put their eating utensils down and their food was going to grow cold. But he continued talking as if he didn't care. "She is beautiful in every way imaginable. We've made up our minds, and so I wanted to announce our engagement." Erica could feel their eyes on her, could hear the noises they made—whether of delight or cautious surprise, she didn't know. But Brock commanded her attention—especially when he pushed out his chair, got down on one knee, and took her hand in his. She looked down, starting to feel a little giddy, caught up in the fake excitement, and that was when she spied the very real ring he was holding poised at the tip of her left-hand ring finger.

Time almost slowed as she assessed the chunk of jewelry he held. It was probably the loveliest ring she'd ever seen—a band of silver or white gold (she couldn't be sure which) with a big solitaire diamond, but the band was accented with tiny diamonds down both sides, and the top looked like two bands of yellow gold were wrapped around the entire ring, in essence, hugging the rest of it. Now that she was ogling it, she couldn't take her eyes off the tiny piece of jewelry. It was big and beautiful without looking gaudy or pretentious, a work of art.

If this had been a real engagement to a man she truly loved, she would have been moved to tears. This gesture had been unexpected and unbelievably romantic, in spite of the fact that she had none of those feelings for this man.

She had to give him credit, though—he was smooth.

There was no controlling the emotions on her face. What he'd done had been so surprising that her reactions were real. Maybe, in his brilliance, that had been his plan all along. If so, it had worked. Without thought, she brought her right hand up to her mouth, covering it, because she couldn't seem to pick up her jaw.

He was a damn fine actor, too…even *she* was almost convinced. The way his cool blue eyes captured a look of sincerity, the genuine sound in his voice of a man smitten, his loving gestures—he was on his game. She knew he'd had plenty of practice doling out emotions meant to seem real but actually completely under his control in the courtroom, but seeing him in action blew her away.

In fact, he was so good that she doubted she'd ever believe anything he said again.

His solid baritone voice was all she could hear when he said the words. The clinking of forks against plates, the piano music wafting overhead, the muted conversation of diners at other tables—all that was gone when Brock said, "Erica, will you make me the happiest man on the planet and say you'll marry me?"

She pushed out of her mind the fact that none of this was real, because his proposal was the kind girls (including a tiny part of her own self) dreamed of. She allowed herself to feel elated and thrilled, and, now that her mouth was once again closed, she felt her lips spread in a wide smile.

As silly as it seemed, he had taken her breath away. How would this compare to a real proposal someday? Would Brock's little act make all genuine suitors' efforts pale in comparison?

She searched his eyes, caught up in a strange feeling of romance for the moment, and she said, "Yes. I would be honored to be your bride."

She'd almost made a mistake. A simple one, but it would have been quite noticeable. Instead of saying *your bride*, she'd almost said, "The future Mrs. Brock Ford," only with his middle name—*which she didn't know*. Whirlwind romance or not, a future spouse would know her mate's middle name. And so she intended to solve that problem later.

Meanwhile, time seemed to speed up again as sounds rushed in. She noticed first Mrs. Ford who had a sweet smile on her face, her hands clasped at her chin as if praying. Erica then felt too uncomfortable to look at anyone else at the table, so she glanced once more at Brock.

Again, so awkward. But would it feel awkward if they were really madly in love?

He got up off his knee and slid back into his seat, but it was seconds later that he kissed Erica on the cheek. She'd had to control herself so that she didn't gasp or let her eyes grow wide, even though his lips on her skin had shocked her at first.

But the lingering scent of his masculine cologne tickled her nostrils, making her mind go places where it really shouldn't.

The kiss made her a little pissed, because he was taking liberties she hadn't given him permission to. It was one thing to pretend to be engaged but quite another to physically act upon it. She'd have to set the record straight later. In the meantime, she had to act like everything was normal.

And maybe that was the only reason why he'd done it—for

believability's sake.

She needed to assess if anyone had caught that she was none too happy with Brock, but—as she glanced around the table—she saw that everyone was still taking in the news. The elder Mr. Ford seemed shocked. Was it because Erica wasn't from money or an influential family in this area of Colorado? But when his mouth spread into a warm grin, she realized it had merely taken him by surprise—just like everyone else at the table.

Which had been what Brock had wanted, so mission accomplished.

Erica allowed herself to look at everyone at the table now and saw that, in spite of everyone seeming a little off their footing (thanks to Brock suddenly ending his perpetual bachelor phase, so far as they knew), they were all accepting of her as his fiancée.

Brock's mother, hands still clasped, asked, "Do you have a date in mind?"

"Nothing set in stone, mom. We're thinking sometime in the spring."

"Oh, dear. You haven't given us much time to plan anything."

Well, if only she knew… Erica said, "We just don't want to wait. And we're wanting to do something really simple."

"Come on, mom. It's up to the bride's parents to cover the wedding anyway." Brock put his arm around Erica and pulled her close. "We're not too worried about all that. It'll all work out."

Erica forced a smile but wondered how long she'd have to put up with how handsy he was being. If he thought he could play around like that and get away with it, he had another think coming. The kiss on the cheek and snuggling—that hadn't been part of the bargain. She was going to have to set him straight ASAP.

She survived. Brady Ford gave a long speech about his illustrious career and the family he loved, adding how proud he was that his sons had all chosen to follow in his footsteps. Then a friend chose to say something about Mr. Ford and how happy he was that he'd be enjoying life after law. And then it was a lovefest. The mike was passed from one person to another and another and another…and then Erica thought she might get sick. Yes, Brock's father seemed like a decent guy, but surely even he was growing tired of the ass kissing.

Whispering to Brock that she had to get a little fresh air, she tried to be discreet about leaving their table. Even though all the action was focused on the other end, she couldn't be sure she wasn't obvious and definitely didn't want to offend anyone just because she was getting up for a few moments. But it looked like she could get away with it with no harm done.

She had finally made her way out of the dining room to the reception area and felt like she could breathe a little. Did she want to go to the ladies' restroom or get her coat and step outside? There was no chance to decide, because Brock showed up, placing a hand on her upper arm.

"Everything okay?"

"Peachy. I just needed a few minutes." No better time than the present, though. "But we need to chat for a second. Why don't you follow me?"

Brock's lovely dark brows furrowed over his eyes, making him look roguishly handsome—part of the reason she needed to talk with him.

"Is anything wrong?"

"Actually, yes." They walked toward the restroom area and sat on a nearby bench. Erica made sure to keep her voice low so they wouldn't blow their cover. "I get that we need to convince your family, but I think we already have."

"What do you mean?"

"The kiss on the cheek. The arm around my shoulders. Was all that necessary?"

Brock cocked a lovely eyebrow, making it hard for her to stand firm. "That's what loving premarital couples do. They express affection. If we act like third graders at a dance, no one will buy it."

"I realize that—but it doesn't change the fact that you're getting a little too cozy. Your hand around my waist walking in was fine. Kissing me on the cheek was pushing it." No way in hell was she going to tell him that, in spite of everything repulsive about him, she also found him incredibly sexy and almost irresistible. If he didn't keep his hands to himself, she was going to *want* him to touch her—and that would be bad all the way around.

"Look, I did it for believability."

"Bullshit," she said, a little more firmly than she'd meant to. She inhaled slowly and then added, more calmly, "Hands off."

He raised his eyebrows—and then his hands—before saying, "Fine." As he relaxed his back, he added, "You *will* be a great trial lawyer."

"Thanks...I think." She glanced around, making sure they were still alone. "By the way, if we're engaged to be married, I should probably know your middle name, don't you think? Mine's Renee."

"Andrew." He lowered his voice more and then said, "And I might as well tell you—when this is over, you can keep the ring."

"What?"

"Yes. Consider it my thanks."

"Are you crazy? This had to have cost thousands of dollars."

A smirk covered Brock's smug face. "You have no idea. But it's the least I can do. Just keep it and don't argue with me."

Erica wasn't sure if she liked or hated his bossy side. Whatever the case, her sexual side hadn't gotten the memo that no decision had been made yet, because it was warming up to the man quite nicely, bossy or not.

"And what about when your parents ask if you got it back?"

"They won't." After a moment, he added, "Bret's more likely to do that than they are."

She held her left hand out, splaying the fingers to admire the ring. "It really *is* beautiful."

"It is, isn't it? It fits okay?"

"Perfectly. How did you know?" A sly grin was the only answer she was going to get for that question, and it didn't take long for her to realize that. "How did you pick it out?"

His smile muted, feeling a little less playful, a little more genuine. "I look for something unique—and, when I find it, I usually have to own it."

Erica might have refrained from rolling her eyes, but after hearing comments like that, she was definitely glad she wasn't going to be marrying this boor. "We should probably get back now, don't you think?"

"I suppose...but don't think for a second that I'll be enjoying it any more than you will."

She *did* doubt it, but her lips were sealed.

*   *   *

Dessert wasn't half bad, but crème brûlée had always been a little too rich for him. After all the other food, the ending note was a bit much…and it only made him want to have an after-dinner drink.

But Bret and Brandon both asked if Brock could come with them for a few minutes. The women at the table all turned toward Erica, so he hoped she'd do okay on her own without him there as backup, but when he spied Helen Shockley, a rich bitch who pushed money toward things she wanted to influence, he knew that she'd distract the shit out of his mother and possible Elle, too—meaning Erica would likely do just fine.

The three brothers wound up in another area of the expansive restaurant where there was a bar. Bret ordered them all shots and, while they waited, Brandon took a box out of his jacket pocket. "We got this for dad. You can pay us your share later."

"What is it?"

Brandon's grin was infectious. "A gold watch. What else?"

Brock looked over the watch face, recognizing the name Audemars Piguet on the face, realizing that damn watch likely cost more than some people made in a lifetime. It was certainly worth more than his first three cars combined. "That set you back a pretty penny."

"*Us*. But dad's worth it."

The watch wasn't exactly gold but a rosy gold tone, something unique their father would appreciate, even if he never wore it. The bartender delivered their shots and Bret gave the man his credit card. Brock didn't waste any time slamming the drink, trying to figure out how much his portion would be for the watch.

But why the hell was he worried? He was getting ready to inherit a third of his father's firm. He'd be bringing home even more money now—possibly half a mil a year or more. This watch was a mere token of the kind of cash he'd showered with.

Brock didn't see it, but Bret ordered a second round and then both his brothers asked him to have a seat. The bar wasn't crowded, because it served the restaurant that was also running the party they'd ditched. There were two couples nursing drinks, probably waiting for their table to clear, and the bartender was taking care of them but mostly wiping the bar with a pristine white piece of terrycloth.

The three brothers huddled at a table in the corner, away from everyone else, and Brandon said, "There's something else we need to talk with you about, but I'm not sure—"

"Oh, *I'm* sure," Bret said, interrupting their middle sibling. Staring Brock down, he said, "I don't know what the hell is up your sleeve, Brock, but we're calling bullshit."

"What do you mean?" Brock knew his face looked completely innocent, guileless, guilt-free, and maybe even a little confused that his brothers would even deign to accuse him of something…whatever it was, even if he was fairly certain he knew what they were talking about. But they would never know it from his face. It was a look perfected for the courtroom: a visage of complete innocence that said, *I know nothing.*

Bret's lids lowered but his voice did not. His tone hadn't been loud to begin with, and there would be no chance that the people around them would have overheard unless they'd been straining with the intention of eavesdropping. "You know damn good and well what I mean. You're all of a sudden engaged to Erica Larson…my direct *employee*. Why is this the first time we've heard you're even dating her?"

Brock pasted on the perfect smirk. "Come on, Bret. Do you really think you know everything that goes on at the firm? You leave the office no later than six o'clock every evening—and earlier when Elle has something planned for the two of you." He turned his attention to Brandon. "And that goes double for you. You're out of there by five-thirty at the latest, and that's provided there's nothing going on with Lisa or the baby. Did you know there are some nights that Erica's been there past nine, and the cleaning crew has her leave when they do so they can arm the building?"

Ah, it was working. They were deer in headlights. He'd been calling their bluff. Honestly, he had no idea if they knew Erica's work habits, so he'd been testing the water—and discovered they didn't pay close enough attention.

So he turned back to Bret. "And you're her boss. You know nothing about her."

Unfortunately for Brock, even though Bret was no litigator, he was still sharp as a tack and clever as hell. The sour look on his face communicated ongoing disbelief. "I'd venture that you don't know much about her, either."

Brock raised his eyebrows. "I know a hell of a lot more than you do." His eyes moved between his brothers before returning to Bret. "Here's something you should know, considering *you* hired her. What's her middle name?"

"Like I would remember that."

"It's part of her employment agreement, Bret. And I thought you had an eye for detail."

Brandon was shaking his head. "That's not fair, Brock. She was part of that big hiring stint we did when you were involved in the Rocky Mountain Data Solutions trial. We hired at least a dozen people. How could we remember one person's name?"

"It's Renee." He owed the girl a kiss for that one—not that she'd take it. "And make all the excuses you want." Now that he'd turned the table, he planned to be relentless. "It's information you would know if you paid attention."

Bret was frowning and opened his mouth to talk.

But Brock beat him to it—if he didn't maintain surprise, he could drop the ball. "Here's the bottom line, guys. You're just jealous because I'm dating a beautiful young woman who can take care of herself. You're already trapped in loveless, boring marriages with tired old women who are sick of your shit." He didn't believe any of it. He knew his brothers adored their wives and those women were *not* tired or old. But he was on the defense, and nothing and no one was sacred when it came to protecting his client. Tonight, *he* was the guilty guy he was defending.

"That's not fair," Bret said. "We—"

A guy from the firm's billing unit appeared out of nowhere, slapping Bret on the back. "Your dad was looking for all of you."

The look on his oldest brother's face was priceless. And Brock felt his muscles relax as he realized the suspicion was deflected. Well…maybe not the suspicion but being accused to his face. And he'd passed the first test with flying colors.

Just to be safe, though, maybe he needed ask Erica when her birthday was…

CHAPTER FIVE

BROCK KNEW HIS brothers were far from convinced that he and Erica had been dating. They saw right through him *and* they knew why. It had been an unspoken thing, but it had been as loud as a tornado siren: only married brothers would get to run the firm. Bret and Brandon had been convinced they'd be shutting out their little brother—the rebel, the troublemaker, the one who always fought their perfect plans—and now they were getting ready to lose the power they hadn't inherited in the first place.

The three brothers would continue to be equals…and he knew that pissed them off.

He was fairly certain from the reactions earlier that his parents had bought it, but if his brothers had doubts, his mother and father might have some sense of disbelief as well. He needed to quash those reservations now before his brothers nurtured the seed they were tending in their own gardens.

There was one quick and easy way to do it.

The trio of brothers approached the long table where they'd eaten dinner, and it was obvious by the way their father was looking at the three men that he had wanted to talk with them. Brock noticed that a small musical ensemble had set up on the dance floor area and were getting ready to play. Yes, heaven forbid they let the night end early and send everyone to bed with full bellies.

He had court tomorrow.

Nothing a little caffeine wouldn't take care of, he supposed, and, in all fairness, this party was unusual. The attorneys he knew weren't accustomed to celebrating this way anyway. When he won a trial, he'd have some drinks, find a good lay (one who would shut her mouth by midnight or, better yet, wouldn't be butt hurt if he went home), and be back at it the next day.

This…this, though, was his mother's doing and his father was only too happy to oblige. He'd handed her the checkbook and told her to go to town.

And here they were.

If it hadn't been for all this, Brock probably wouldn't have met Erica and most definitely wouldn't have known her middle name. Not that it mattered. It was Shakespeare who'd said a rose would smell as sweet, no matter what the name. A woman like Erica would be just as beautiful—and just as feisty—no matter the name her parents bestowed upon her. Pretending to be in love with her was easy.

With that thought weighing heavily on his mind, he strode over to the table and touched Erica's arm—on the inside just above the elbow—and it got her attention, just as he'd hoped. She turned slightly and he knew he couldn't hesitate. He pulled her close to him and consumed her mouth. It wasn't going to be the first kiss girls dreamed of—sweet, soft, and gentle. Instead, it was going to be possessive and lusty-looking…but it was all for show. Yes, he knew she'd be angry, but she'd get over it.

He knew what was at stake here.

As his mouth touched hers, though, their lips ignited. *Holy fuck.* This was something he hadn't expected—a huge spark between them. He touched her tongue with his then—completely unnecessary per his plan—but now that he was committed, he couldn't stop himself, any more than he could stop the snow from falling come winter. She tasted sweet, like nectar from the most delicate pink flower, but all he could think of was sin. Now that he was suckling her lips, he could feel a burning desire to consume all of her.

He didn't know how he could convince her of that, though, because she wasn't like one of his usual conquests.

She didn't want him.

He felt her fingernails digging into the flesh at the base of his neck. That was her way of telling him to stop right now without his family knowing, and she might have thought it would deter him. Unfortunately, the way she was cutting his flesh was fucking hot and having the exact opposite effect on him than she'd wanted.

He only stopped kissing her when he was damn good and ready.

Pulling his lips off hers, he opened his eyes. Her hand was still clenched around his neck, but she seemed almost short of breath...and she took her sweet time opening her eyes.

His smile was likely close to a smirk, too, but at least she didn't slap his face. "I missed you, honey," he said. And all he cared about was that his family found his performance credible.

Without reasonable doubt.

Now he had to present a case to himself in his own head to convince himself not to pursue this woman in earnest. As good an attorney as he was, he didn't know that he could pull it off.

What the hell was that?

Brock was going to get an earful when they were alone. She'd just lectured him about kissing her on the cheek, so it was like he'd upped the ante. What had he been thinking?

She couldn't very well take him away and chew his butt, though, because his father had summoned the brothers. They had left the table earlier, thinking all the pomp and circumstance was over. Technically, it was, because all the gushing and grandstanding at the microphone had stopped and now a few couples swayed on the dance floor. Erica thought that was nuts, because she wanted to go home and curl up with a nice warm brief to put her to sleep while she examined what evidence she'd have to dig up tomorrow.

"Thank you for coming back, my sons. I wanted to spend a little more time with you before we all go on our way."

Bret cleared his throat. "First, dad, we wanted to give you something." The oldest brother got close to their father and pulled out a small silver box with a shimmery bow. How it had stayed looking fresh in his pocket, Erica would never know. As Bret handed Brady Ford the box, he said, "Dad, we wanted to thank you—for all the years of instruction, of encouragement, even of discipline as you created us to be the men we are today. We wouldn't be here if not for you and our beautiful mother. We want to wish you the best as you begin the next phase of your life. And, since they always talk about gold watches at retirement..." His voice faded as he handed the box to the eldest Ford, whose face beamed, not just with pride but with satisfaction that his sons held him in such high esteem.

"Oh, my sons," Brady said as he admired the expensive watch he took out of the package to admire. He handed it to Harper who examined it at length. "I can't tell you how proud all three of you make me. Please be seated."

Everyone at the table, without exception, did as the older man asked. "I suppose I need to tell you my plans. I'm not certain when I'll leave—some time over the next year, to be sure—but I want to make sure all three of you feel comfortable with running the firm once I'm no longer at the helm. While I'm not running away and can always be called for consultations, I have no further desire to practice law. I've done all the great things I'd wanted to do and now I'm ready to play and have fun." He looked over at his wife and winked. "Actually, your mother and I both do. We want to travel the world and play a little before we have more grandkids and they get older and want more of our time. In fact, we're considering a second home somewhere—Hawaii, France, or the Bahamas—while enjoying summers here in Colorado."

The man went on and on, detailing some of his plans, and Erica didn't have to try to tune him out. She was still furious over Brock's stolen kiss. In fact, she was halfway tempted right this second to blow his cover and expose their ruse...but then she'd be able to kiss her new job away. She was still stuck in research, although Brock had promised their announcement would change that. Time would tell.

Her ire continued to grow as she realized something else: she could still feel his lips on hers, as if they'd been coated with cinnamon or peppermint. The nerves of that skin felt tingly and, as she imagined his tongue in her mouth, she licked her bottom lip, forcing herself not to smile.

Wow. Deep down, she knew she wanted more. Much more.

She could have kissed Brock Ford all night long and not grown tired of it.

When she realized Brady was continuing to talk, she forced herself to pay attention. "It does our hearts good to know that each of our sons has found someone to spend his life with. I know you all balked at the idea at first, but I think you've all come around. Love is what makes the world go around, boys, and when you find the woman who lights your fire, don't let her go. It's her—and your family—that will fuel your desire to work, long after your clients have worn you out and you've lost joy and passion for what you do."

Erica felt her heart sink a little. What a pessimistic way to look at life—and at the job she'd been working so hard to get. They wouldn't even let her do the job she'd gone to school for, and here was Brady Ford lecturing his offspring to get a wife so they'd work a job it sounded like they'd grow to hate.

No wonder his youngest son decided he had to move into the realm of deception.

It was then that she heard her name. The elder Mr. Ford had been speaking to her and she'd completely missed it. "I'm sorry, sir. What was that again?"

"I asked if you like what you're doing back at the office."

She had to be careful here...didn't want to upset the boss. "Well, I'm doing research—mainly looking for precedent in past tort cases. I work under Bret. And I realize it's a necessary evil."

"I hope he appreciates you. Research can never be underestimated."

"Actually, dad...Bret, I had wanted to talk with you about that."

Erica had to suppress a laugh, because she knew exactly what Brock was doing. Like a true litigator, he was saying something the jury wasn't supposed to hear, but even if he was overruled, the information was still out there. Erica suspected his father would want to know what he had to say, even if Bret asked to discuss it later.

Which he did. "Why don't we leave the office at the office? Tonight is all about dad."

"Yes, and it's still my firm until I sign it over." His tone alone made everyone at the table feel as though they'd been reprimanded. Then his eyes shifted to Brock. "You were saying?"

"Erica's talent is being wasted on research we could have a paralegal doing. No offense to my brothers, but if I'd been part of their interview committee, I wouldn't have squandered Erica's talents like they are. We need to test her skills in civil rights law. That's the kind of thing she's interested in."

"Hmm." Brady looked over at Bret, and Erica knew that meant he regarded his oldest son as his right-hand man. Maybe that was why Bret was literally sitting in that position at the table. "Should we maybe have her shadow Seng?"

Brock intervened, however. "Actually...I would like to train her myself."

Bret scoffed. "You're the farthest thing there is from civil rights law."

"No matter what her focus is, she needs to learn how to construct an ironclad argument. She needs to learn to negotiate. I've got that in the bag."

Brandon, raising his voice to be heard from the other end of the table, said, "I don't think she should work directly with you because it smacks of nepotism."

Brock let out a hearty chuckle. "That's rich, Bran. Didn't you shadow dad for a few months fresh out of law school? If that's not nepotism, I don't know what is."

The eldest Ford's hand landed on the table—it wasn't so much a slap as it was a jostle, just enough to get everyone's attention. "Brock is serious about law. And he's right. Consider it done." He looked over at Erica and she could see by the way his boys obeyed that he was viewed as stern and strict, but his brown eyes were kind and warm as he viewed her. She wasn't sure what she'd done to deserve it, but she got the feeling that she and Brady Ford would get along famously. Now if she could get his youngest son to keep his hands and lips to himself, this charade might be a piece of cake.

They were out in traffic and hadn't spoken while Brock navigated the traffic lights. In spite of the fact that it was later in the evening, there were still plenty of cars on the road. New York might have been the city that never slept, but Denver didn't snooze, either. It just got darker—but at least there was no chance of traffic jams this time of the evening.

Erica could still feel Brock's lips on hers, and that pissed her off. This man whom she should despise shouldn't have been taking up so much real estate in her brain. "I suppose I should thank you for getting me out of research."

"You're welcome."

God, his voice dripped with cockiness. That, too, pissed her off.

And turned her on at the same time.

Which made her all the angrier.

"But I also need to ask you why the hell you kissed me? That wasn't part of the bargain, Brock."

As the car whirred down the well-lit street, the lights above them kept the inside of the vehicle bright enough that she could see the smirk on his face. *Dammit.* She was drawn to and repulsed by him at the same time. Talk about confusing. "You seemed to have liked it."

"Seriously, Brock. You can't do that. If this charade can't be pulled off without your mitts all over me, maybe we need to break off the engagement right now. After all, didn't you get what you wanted?"

"Look, I know the kiss wasn't part of the bargain—but my brothers weren't buying it. They were onto me from the get go, and they told me as much. So, yeah, I can argue it all I want, but I had to convince them. And, if nothing else, I had to convince my parents, and kissing you publicly was the easiest way I could think of. That way, when Bret and Brandon go whining to my dad about how I shouldn't be given my fair share of controlling interest in the firm, he can tell them to zip it because I'm engaged."

Erica hated to admit it had probably worked. "Fine. But you could at least apologize. You didn't even ask my permission."

He glanced over at her before returning his eyes to the road. "I didn't hurt you, did I?"

"No." He *wasn't* going to say sorry, was he? Her eyes were glowering but she clamped her jaw shut, reminding herself that, at least, she was going to get to *really* practice law soon—probably as soon as tomorrow.

"My parents like you. Dad really took a shine to you." Why that made Erica feel warm and squishy, she didn't know, because it wasn't like these people were truly going to be in-laws. It was all a sham, and she'd do well to remember that. "It's going to break their hearts when we call off our engagement." Brock merged onto the freeway like a Nascar driver—in complete control but fast as hell.

She'd never admit his car made him hotter...but she also

suspected he already knew it.

"But it has to be done. They put me in this situation, and I'm doing what I have to do."

As Brock drove south, they were bathed more in darkness than they had been downtown, and Erica was alone with her thoughts. At first, she'd maybe felt a little sympathy that Brock was going to be shut out of the family fortune if he wasn't married, but now it didn't seem quite like that. No...he just wouldn't have as much power as he'd wanted. And, to get it, he was willing to deceive everyone he said he loved. This guy, her supposed fiancé, was all about the money and power, and she suspected he would do anything for both.

Those qualities made Brock Andrew Ford, Attorney at Law, dangerous—and the epitome of the kind of man Erica would never want. So why the hell did this guy turn her on so much?

Although they'd chatted some, the drive home was mostly spent in silence. And, thanks to picking her up earlier in the evening, Brock didn't even need to ask her for directions to her place.

So it was dead quiet in the car for most of the trip.

It had to be because she was still angry at him for the kiss. He'd known she'd be upset, but maybe she was the type of woman to carry a grudge and be angry for days. Well, she could throw her little silent treatment tantrum. It wasn't like he was planning on marrying her in reality anyway.

When he pulled into a parking space in the quiet lot, he said, "I'll walk you to your door."

Erica already had her purse in hand, her fingers on the door handle. "Don't bother."

"I insist." Yes, she was probably safe, but if he'd intended on merely dropping her off, he would have pulled the car to the front of the building. Real fiancée or not, it was in his best interest to keep her safe.

But she was going to have to get used to him, like it or not.

She was too quick for him to open the door for her and let her out, but he was walking beside her when he pointed the key fob behind him to lock the car. And they could have walked the entire distance in silence, but he wasn't going to let that happen. "I know you're angry, Erica." She started to shake her head. "There's no sense in denying it. I'm sorry, okay?" As they walked under a street light, he thought he saw her features soften a bit. "I did what I had to do—and the kiss sealed the deal."

Frowning, she said, "Fine. Apology accepted. But *don't* do it again."

"I make no promises." She glared at him as they approached the front doors of the complex.

"Good night, Brock." The disdain with which his name dripped from her mouth gave him chills.

And made him want to possess her.

"What—you're not inviting me up? Isn't that what engaged people do?"

Her hand on the door, she turned, her words full of venom. "You can kiss my ass."

He was still grinning, amused and intrigued, as he walked back to his car, a spring in his step.

He would have to make Erica Larson his—even though that plan was likely the most dangerous one he'd concocted in a very long time.

CHAPTER SIX

BY THE TIME Sunday rolled around, Erica would have thought she'd have news to report to Camilla, but no such luck. Erica was in the basement of her apartment complex, folding the laundry from two different dryers, talking to her best friend through the speaker on her cell phone. Although she was able to tell her all about Brady Ford's retirement party, the rest of her week had been rather lackluster.

"So I was sure with all their talk about my talent and not wanting to relegate me to research, Thursday morning I'd be packing up my junk and moving."

"Do you want my advice, Erica?" Camilla paused. "Or are you just needing to vent?"

She let out a long breath of air. "Eh…I don't know."

Her friend chuckled. "Okay, then I'll give you my opinion and you can take it or leave it."

"Okay."

"You need to be forceful. Let them have it. They made you a promise and now they're reneging. You're the lawyer—isn't that a breach of contract or something?"

"Well, in all fairness, Brock has been by my desk a couple of times. He said they were in negotiations about where to locate me."

"In negotiations? Like it's a major peace treaty?"

Erica thought back to Wednesday night, recalling the rivalry amongst the brothers. Brock was the youngest, a black sheep rebel who stood out because of the work he did and didn't seem to care about love or affection or good will—but he *did* want his damn place in the company. Bret and Brandon both seemed to be hell bent on making sure Brock didn't get a piece of the pie unless he'd met the conditions set forth by their father. "Actually, yes. It very well might be."

"Really? That bad?"

"Yes." Erica proceeded to tell her friend about how Brock had surprised her with a sensual kiss. Just thinking about it flooded her with emotion, reminding her just how much she'd enjoyed it despite her better judgment. But that secret was going with her to the grave. There was no way she was going to let a soul know just how much her body desired Brock Ford, because her brain knew that falling for him would be setting herself up for heartbreak. A guy like that who wanted to play the field forever? A guy who loved the adrenaline of driving fast and warring in the courtroom? And heaven knew what other things got him off.

Brock Ford might have been sexy as hell, smelled and tasted delicious, and flipped a few of her switches, but he was *not* boyfriend material.

And definitely not a husband.

Perhaps she was already building her case for the big breakup that would come later.

"That's what I would have done."

Oh, *shit*. She was tuning out again, just like she had the other night when Brady had been talking to her. "I'm sorry. What was that?"

"I said I would have slapped him."

"Yes, but that would have blown our cover." She giggled. "I *did* think about grinding the heel of my shoe into his foot. But here's the part that's really gonna make you roll your eyes."

"Yeah?"

"Yeah. He invited himself up to my apartment."

"What? What did you say?"

"No, of course. But I have to tell you…if he's as good in bed as he is a kisser, we could have had a good time."

"Oh, God. You *should* have."

"No way. He's a player. Not going there. Besides, with this deal, I'm just this side of a hooker anyway."

"No! If he's making you feel that way *now*—and you haven't

even gotten out of the bargain what you were supposed to—how are you going to feel by the time you're done?"

Erica shook her head. "No, Cam. I don't feel slutty or anything. And no more used now than I did a couple of weeks ago slaving away with no end in sight." She glanced down at her left hand, now laden with the beautiful ring that was just shy of gaudy, and said, "I forgot to tell you, though. He actually proposed to me in front of his family."

"What?!"

"Yes! He got down on one knee and slid this amazing ring on my finger. He even had the size right. If I'd really been engaged to him, I might have swooned. It's got to be worth thousands of dollars. I have no clue how much it costs."

"What if you lose it?"

"Actually, he said I could keep it."

"Seriously? You should have it appraised."

"I'll wait. If I don't get out of this what was promised, I might need a little money while I consider my options." Erica took a deep breath, looking away from the sparkling jewelry on her finger. "It's been so long since I started working there, I can hardly remember exactly why I chose Ford & Associates over the other two firms who made me offers, but I think it was because they were smaller and so I was sure I had a good chance of being a big fish in a little pond. I'd started doubting it until Brock presented me with this crazy offer. I just want them to get the ball rolling like they promised so I can start living my lawyer dream."

"Well, I'd blame that on Brock, the guy who said he'd make it happen in exchange for your acting services. Between his lack of delivering and him thinking he can stick his tongue and dick in you just because you're playing his fiancée make me think you need to rattle his cage. I mean…he obviously doesn't respect you like he should. I say you set the record straight tomorrow by demanding what they promised."

When Erica marched into Ford & Associates on Monday morning, she was on a warpath just as Camilla had fired her up to be. Sometimes Erica thought maybe Camilla should have been the lawyer because her sense of justice was not only as strong as

Erica's, but Camilla often seemed more prone to action, while Erica preferred to think about it long enough to be sure she was making a sound decision.

But that was often why she bounced things off her friend—because Cam always gave good advice and she was a great listener.

So Erica was wearing a black suit from head to toe. At Camilla's suggestion, she was wearing a pant suit, not one with a skirt. She wanted to come across as an equal rather than a subordinate and playing against gender roles was one way to do that.

But when she texted Brock on her way in and he told her he wouldn't be in until nine because he had an out-of-office meeting, she stewed—and then she decided to treat herself to Starbucks. A little sweetness would help her keep her cool until he arrived.

And it worked. She settled into the mind-numbing research once more, finding it all too easy. Off and on, she could hear Camilla's voice in her head, and she assured that voice that she would get her say—but she'd have to wait.

It wasn't until close to ten that morning that Brock arrived at her little desk tucked in a corner, a place where she hadn't actually worked since her first month or so in the firm, preferring to spread out on the first-floor conference room table. It was cramped in her cubicle, located amongst lots of other first and second year lawyers, as well as clerks and paralegals. Her space belied her title and salary and thinking about it irritated her to no end. Had Brock arrived any later, he might have had to deal with her wrath.

When she looked up, he had his classic smirk plastered on his face. His blue eyes were sparkling, his teeth whiter than usual...and she felt her heart leap in her chest, even though her ire should have been bubbling in her throat. She swallowed, trying to figure out what to say next, but his words took her off guard.

"Do you prefer mountain scenes or something avant garde?"

"What does that even mean?"

"The artwork in your new office. I was trying to decide the finishing touches and figured I should let *you* do that—since you'll be the one spending the time in there." She cocked an eyebrow, feeling like he was dangling another nonexistent carrot. "You wanna see it?"

"What? Artwork?"

"No—your office."

She couldn't help the surge of happiness that rushed through her veins. It was real. "Of course."

"Let's go." Gladly. She picked up the paper cup and stood, ready to follow wherever he led. "Nice suit, by the way."

Ah, he noticed—but he didn't know why she'd worn it, and that would remain her little secret. They walked out past the reception desk into the lobby, but he didn't lead her toward the stairs. He walked over to the elevator and pushed the up arrow. Glancing over at her while they waited, he asked, "What are you drinking?"

"Starbucks."

His eyes told her he was not amused with her terse answer. "I can *see* that."

"It's white mocha," she said, taking a sip from the venti-sized cup.

"Why do you drink that stuff? You know it's not good for you."

The fight she'd stored up for demanding Brock make good on his promises channeled its way into her arguments for Starbucks. "It's nice to know that you're health conscious, but let me worry about my own well-being. I'm not suffering from the occasional coffee."

He arched an eyebrow, looking devilishly handsome.

Dammit.

Brock also appeared to be in fantastic shape, meaning he probably *did* pay attention to those kinds of things.

"Okay, fair enough, but if you love yourself, you should avoid all the sugar and fat in those drinks."

"I don't know why you're suddenly worried about my well-being, Brock. Lattes are one of the few joys I have in life. In fact, I'd say Starbucks was the *only* sweet thing in my life while I was slaving away over piles of work here for the past year. See, I came here thinking I was going to be working my dream job after all those years in college and instead got stuck doing the shit work no one else wanted to do. I get that I've been paying my dues, but I wanted some bit of happiness—and Starbucks represented that." The elevator *dinged* as it stopped at the top floor. "Did *you* have to go through all that—paying your dues here?"

"No, not in the sense you are."

She was fired up and her mouth was speeding along faster

than her brain. "Ha. You're a spoiled rich boy who had it all handed to him."

It wasn't until the doors opened that Erica realized they were on the third floor. She'd expected an office on the second...and here she was bitching about her fate with the firm. At the moment, she was looking a gift horse in the mouth.

There was a desk just as they walked out of the elevator, and a woman sat in front of a computer, typing away. Erica knew she was the lead secretary on that floor, also a bit of an office manager, and she was placed there to direct people where they needed to go—including back downstairs, if they were lost.

As Brock led the way to the right in silence, she thought maybe she'd bested him, but once they were out of earshot of the secretary—in spite of the fact that anyone could be coming down the hall at any moment—he said, "You're sadly mistaken, Erica. I earned every little damn thing I got. I busted my ass to get to where I am." He paused at a doorway and motioned with his hand, indicating that she should step inside. "If you'd prefer it that way—working your way up from the bottom—we can arrange that."

She felt pissed at him then, because he couldn't even see how his ass busting was so much different from hers—but, looking inside the space that she presumed would be her new office, she knew she should be grateful that she had this opportunity.

But what she was having to do to get it...

Trying to stop herself from looking around the space, imagining herself in there at the beautiful mahogany desk, surrounded by old-fashioned law books with a Persian rug underneath and tasteful decorations filling the space with her own sensibilities (much more complex than a mountain painting versus avant garde), she focused her eyes on the man she was pretending to want to marry. Yes, whether he saw it or not, he'd been born with a silver spoon in his mouth, and his version of climbing to the top was a hell of a lot easier than hers had been—or would continue to be. Not only did he have the advantage of being the owner's son, he was a man, which also made things lots easier for him in this world—but she knew she was in a sweet position...so long as she could keep her mouth shut and be a good little girl.

She actually wanted to *practice* law.

So she took in a long slow breath, looking at the man in front

56

of her. Why had she found him so damn sexy a few minutes ago? At this moment, she was repulsed. But she had to keep that to herself. "I feel like I already have." Finally, she allowed herself to really look around the space. There was a beautiful view of Lakewood just outside the huge window. The room itself was boring, aside from the monstrous desk, complete with computer and phone—freshly painted white walls and beige carpeting—but the potential was amazing. She could definitely see herself in there doing the work she'd envisioned all those years ago.

She couldn't read his voice when he said, "There are still a couple of things that will be moved in here—shelving and chairs for your clients—but I wanted to let you see it. And, if you're ready, I'll have you sitting with me for the rest of the morning."

Her soul suddenly felt light, making her almost feel bad for being nasty a few moments ago.

Almost.

"I'm definitely ready." Should she even ask? "Am I moving up here for good?"

"Yes. Tomorrow morning, you'll want to move any personal belongings from your space downstairs to up here. And I believe Bret said to let Linda know where you are in the work you're doing."

She wracked her brain, trying to remember who Linda was—a clerk, a fellow attorney, a paralegal downstairs in the sea of cubicles from which she was being rescued? But then she remembered Linda was one of Bret's secretaries. She nodded her head in affirmation.

"In the meantime, today you'll be sitting with me as I meet with clients. I have a full calendar of appointments this afternoon, including a client I need to prep for a trial next week." Erica nodded. Nothing had been happening and now all of a sudden, she had to focus to keep up. "What are your plans for Thanksgiving?"

That was odd. "Umm…I think that's personal."

Brock raised a gorgeous eyebrow and his dimples appeared in his cheeks. Holy shit. This guy was to die for. Too bad most of the things that came out of his mouth made her *want* to die. "Yes, you're absolutely right. And, in case you've forgotten, we're engaged and should be privy to that sort of thing."

She felt the air leak out of her lungs. This whole thing was becoming a hell of a lot more complicated than she'd wanted. "I usually spend some time with my family, even if it's only the actual holiday."

"And where are my future in-laws?"

Was it strange to find it creepy that he seemed to be fully embracing the role today? But she only wondered for a moment before Brandon popped his head in the door, his brown hair looking slightly trimmed since she'd last seen him. "Hey, Erica. Like your new digs?"

"Yes, I think so." She was happy that at least Brandon was acting polite instead of giving off the vibes she'd been getting from him during the retirement party.

"Good deal. Hey, bro, you got plans for lunch?"

"Actually, yeah. I'm taking my girl out for sushi at Motomaki."

"I don't do sushi." Oh, shit. Maybe she shouldn't have said that.

Brock recovered quickly. "I keep hoping to talk you into it, honey. You don't have to eat sushi there, even though I'd like you to give it a try. They have other food and I've been wanting to take you there for a while."

Brandon smiled. "You'll love it, Erica. It's one of our favorite places for lunch. Hey—if Bret wants sushi, we can meet you guys there."

Well, that sounded like a lot of fun. The three rival brothers pissing all over each other during lunch. No, thanks—Erica would be just fine with another white mocha latte.

"Look, Bran, as much as I'd love that, Erica and I have wedding plans to discuss."

She jumped on it. When she and Camilla had still been undergrads, they'd talked about the perfect wedding—and she knew all the particulars involved…which was why she didn't know if she even wanted a traditional ceremony anymore. But, for now, she could play the part of excited bride. "Yes—we need to talk color scheme, location, caterer. Oh, and which wedding planner we want to go with."

Brandon's raised eyebrows made his grin look devilish and, for the first time, Erica could see that, in spite of the sibling rivalry, these guys might be nice enough. "Yeah, fair enough. I don't want to go through that stuff again, no matter how long I live."

"What about Saffy? The parents of the bride have to do all that crap."

Brock was wrong and Brandon told him so. "Nope. We only have to foot the bill. And, besides, by then, if Saffy wants that kind of help, Lisa will be more than happy to offer it. I only have to sign the damn checks. Anyway, maybe tomorrow for lunch?"

"Yeah." Once Brandon had left, Brock lowered his voice. "Thanks. I really didn't want to waste a couple of hours with my brothers. But thanks again for almost blowing our cover."

Erica winced. "Sorry. But, as my fiancé, you need to know I don't like sushi." And then it dawned on her why Brock had been talking like that earlier—because passersby might happen to overhear their conversations. Best to be safe.

"So...where were we?"

"Thanksgiving—my family."

Brock nodded. "The firm is closed on Friday and, even though we're open Monday through Wednesday of that week, we're not too busy. Things slow down a bit. My parents have a condo in Vail that they have a timeshare in, and they spend an entire week there during Thanksgiving and another week in June. Even though I'm here Monday through Wednesday, I spend Thursday through Saturday with them every year."

"Well, that doesn't work for me. I need to see my parents— and I might get lucky and see my brother and his family if they make it down to Colorado. I don't care if we're engaged. I'm going home."

"Where *is* home exactly?"

"Gunnison."

Brock's eyes lit up. "Oh, Gunnison's beautiful. And the skiing in Crested Butte is some of the best."

In spite of having grown up there, she'd only ever been skiing once when she was in middle school—and she'd hated it. But she wasn't going to say that out loud.

"Okay, well...like a real couple, why don't we compromise? Would you be up to splitting the time between the two?"

She actually fucking hated the idea...but she hadn't ever been to Vail. And, so long as she could see her mom and dad and recharge in her hometown with the people she loved, she thought she could maybe do it. "Sure, I guess. But I want to see my parents on Thanksgiving proper. My mom makes the best turkey and her rolls are to die for—and I want to help her in the kitchen. Thanksgiving is my favorite holiday—I don't want to miss it."

"Okay. Not a problem. We always go out to eat and there's nothing fancy about that." He slapped his hands together, rubbing them as if he had a scheme in mind. "Let's hammer out the rest of the details over some lunch, shall we?"

Why was everything a negotiation for this man?

And why was she looking forward to having lunch with him?

But, more than that, why did the upcoming long holiday weekend with Brock seem appealing?

What the hell was he doing to her?

CHAPTER SEVEN

ERICA CURLED HER toes in her boots as Brock took the curves coming down Monarch Pass a little faster than she would have liked. Granted, there was no snow on the ground, but it didn't make her any less fearful. The western slope of Monarch didn't seem as dangerous as the eastern side, but she had no idea if Brock had even driven this road before.

Well, if he knew Crested Butte was a great ski area, then he'd likely been this way once or twice.

But, finally, with that last curve, the road sloped and she knew that even if his car got out of control now, they might be able to survive a crash.

Until she looked at the speedometer.

Over eighty-five miles per hour.

"Why are you in such a hurry?" Erica asked, using it as an excuse to turn down the rap CD Brock was listening to.

"I'm not. Believe me. I'm not eager to see the faces of the people whose hearts I'm going to crush a month or two from now."

"Then why are you driving like a bat out of hell?"

"Am I?" Brock looked down at the dash but the vehicle's speed was already slowing as they dashed past Sargents, a little hole in the wall in Saguache County. The good news was that meant she was almost home, less than an hour away.

She was starting to feel excited. She hadn't seen her parents since July—and she needed this. They really did help her recharge

61

in a way no one and nothing else did. Being home, too, in the Gunnison Valley, surrounded by the Rocky Mountains would refresh her like nothing else.

Too bad she had her supposed husband-to-be with her.

She'd already warned her parents, and her mother had sounded shocked that she'd gone from not even dating to being so head over heels that she'd found a man to marry. On their Skype call, her dad had helped progress the lie immensely. "You never know when love is going to take over. When you find the right person, there's no fighting it."

Aw. She'd known her dad was a softie, but wow.

And what would they think about Brock? Hmm.

"I haven't been back to Gunnison in a long time. I've missed it."

Erica cocked her head as Brock took another corner going entirely too fast, and she had to resist the urge to grip the dash. At this rate, he was going to dump them in the icy Gunnison River. "You visit Gunny a lot?"

"Not much, but I spent my undergrad days at Western."

"Ah, Wasted State."

"Yes, I was here to party and to ski—and then I decided maybe being a lawyer wouldn't be such a bad gig after all."

"You didn't decide to do that right off the bat?"

"Hell, no. By the time I graduated high school, Bret was already working for dad and Brandon was applying to pre-law schools. The last thing I wanted to do was what the rest of my family did. But my first-year grades were shit, and of all the core classes I took, nothing really sparked my interest. World History, a little bit, but what kind of job can you get learning history?

"Dad sat me down and told me in no uncertain terms that he wasn't going to pay for my education if I didn't do better. An F, he said, indicated a complete lack of not trying. And he was right. It was the first time in my life I wasn't under my dad's thumb, so I enjoyed myself. A lot. I thought maybe I'd want to go out of state, but my grades prohibited it. So I stuck it out at Western, focusing on pre-law with a minor in poli sci and started getting decent grades, so then I managed to get into Berkeley. For some reason, having dad disappointed in me made me decide I wanted to try harder. And then I was in a play my sophomore year—playing an attorney, if you can believe that. Mom and dad came and, even though it was a bit part, mom said she was so proud of me; dad said if I could do half of what I did onstage, I'd be a hell of a litigator.

"So that became my goal. My brothers are the lawyers who don't like to enter the courtroom. *I* do. It involved theatrics, thinking on your feet, competition, using your brain—all the things I'm good at and like doing."

"When's the last time you were here?"

"It's been five years at least."

"It's changed a little...so be prepared."

"Ah, what I love about Gunnison is the people—and they never change."

Really? Knowing that Brock loved about her hometown exactly the things she'd found endearing brought a human side to him she hadn't seen before. She'd never discovered another town like her birth place, which brought truth to that old saying, "There's no place like home." One of the things she loved the most was the melding of the people there. There were the old "cattlemen," the proud ranchers of the community, and then there were the college kids, lots of tourists and locals alike who appreciated the great outdoors, along with a real creative, artistic element at both the college and in town. It was a unique blending she'd never seen in any other college town and, even though she hadn't attended the university there, she understood the appeal. She would always love it there.

"So you didn't mind the cold?"

Brock laughed. "Well...does anyone *love* it? At least I was able to brag to my brothers that I had survived the Coldest Spot in the Nation." They went to school in DC and California, so I got 'em beat."

"Yeah, Denver's winters have always seemed warm to me. But I don't hear the 'Coldest Spot' hype anymore. I guess it's not as big a deal."

"Doesn't change the fact that it gets damn cold. I don't know that I'd want to live there longer than I did. Forty below is extreme."

"Oh, come on, Brock. Haven't you always heard that whatever doesn't kill you makes you stronger?"

"Yeah, well, don't believe the hype. I prefer to pick my battles, and fighting the cold isn't one of them."

The two of them lapsed back into silence as Brock's car whirred down the highway in the dark. They'd left Denver earlier that evening after dusk, contending with some rush hour traffic, but once they got out of the city, traveling west on 285, the traffic eased up a bit. It wasn't until they were an hour out that they really noticed lighter traffic.

And now, over one hundred miles later, the cars were few and far between. It wasn't that this stretch of Highway 50 didn't have travelers, because it did, but because it was close to ten PM, there weren't many cars around anymore. They'd stopped for a quick bite and a restroom break in Poncha Springs before scaling the mountain, but they'd otherwise made steady progress.

What Erica found most interesting was that they had several instances of silence on the road, but she hadn't found a single one of them to be uncomfortable. When the two of them did talk, it was never about the firm. Instead, they talked about Colorado (where they'd been and where they wanted to go), funny childhood experiences, and favorite movies.

It turned out they both had a soft spot for "It's a Wonderful Life" and the original version of "The Shining." Neither had ever been to the infamous Stanley Hotel where the movie based on Stephen King's book had been filmed but both wanted to visit sometime.

As a joke, Brock had said, "Maybe we could spend our honeymoon there." Erica told him that was a bit gruesome—as much as she loved it, she would want to save that for another occasion. And she also had to give Brock credit—he was incorporating their fake engagement into as much of his imagination as he could, and she supposed that made him a better actor than she.

Slicing through the night and the whirr of tires on asphalt cutting through the muted tunes on the CD player, Brock said, "So tell me about your family. Is there anything I need to know before going in?"

"Hmm. I'm not sure. My dad teaches math at the high school and mom teaches kindergarten, so I can tell you they love kids. I have a brother who's five years older, so even though we love each other, we never did a whole lot together growing up."

"Sounds kind of like my brothers and me. We're all three or four years apart, like my parents weren't in any big hurry to have kids."

"Nothing wrong with that. At least you know you're wanted."

Brock didn't respond at first. When he did, he asked, "Were you a surprise baby?"

"No. Why do you ask?"

"Because you said, 'At least you know you're wanted,' implying that maybe you weren't."

"Oh, no, I didn't mean it that way. I was just kind of thinking out loud—that parents who plan most definitely communicate to their kids that they're wanted, not to imply that surprise babies aren't." Brock started laughing. "What's so funny?"

"Just thinking about that term. A surprise baby to a couple is a lot different from a surprise baby discovered via paternity test. And I don't know that those parents are that thrilled."

"You never know."

Another minute passed before Brock asked, "Do you want to have kids?"

"Someday. I'm not ready yet."

"Me, either. I like my niece, so I'm pretty sure I'd enjoy kids, but they tie you down. I'll need to get my mind in the right place for that."

"Yeah. I hope I can be the kind of parent my mom and dad were—loving, even though they were a little strict, kind, and fun. They encouraged me to do whatever it was I wanted and supported me along the way. I can only hope to be half as attentive as they were."

"You're lucky." Brock didn't elaborate and Erica was afraid to ask. It seemed to be a sensitive subject, based on his tone. But she wouldn't disagree with him—she was quite fortunate to have such wonderful parents...and she was trying not to focus on the fact that she was only going to see them for little more than twenty-four hours before heading over to spend time with Brock's family. Next year, "single" again, she could spend the entire time with them, but for now, she had to keep reminding herself that what she was doing allowed her to practice her dream job—and she knew her parents would wish nothing less for her.

She only hoped she'd be able to maintain this façade in their presence. Time would tell.

* * *

In spite of his family's wealth, Brock had never been much for appearances. Erica's family could have been living in a double-wide trailer and he wouldn't have thought twice about it.

They didn't, though. They lived in a rustic-looking home on the west side of town. Brock enjoyed driving through Gunnison, because every block brought back memories of his days as a young man out on his own for the first time.

The Larsons lived in a neighborhood, but it was a little out of the town proper. Erica guided the way and they were there less than five minutes after passing Main Street.

While they were getting their luggage out of the trunk, he said, "We're going to have to stop by Mario's on the way out of town Friday."

"You miss their pizza?"

"No, I want a calzone."

"I love their salads, so I guess it's a date."

"I think if we leave after lunch, we should be able to get to Vail by nightfall."

He'd never tell her so, but he would have much rather spent the entire time here with *her* parents—provided they were nice enough. He suspected they were, because they say the apple never falls far from the tree, and if Erica was anything like her parents, he was going to like them.

Her parents must have heard the car doors closing, because Brock could hear a man's voice in the distance saying, "Yes, they're here."

After just those few moments, Brock was feeling the chill seeping through his jeans into his bones, and his nose was getting a good jolt of it as well. Still not as cold as he knew it could and would get, but fall was preparing for winter here. As he set Erica's rolling suitcase on the ground, extending the handle before handing it off to her, he commented, "It's got to be close to freezing."

"Guess you should've worn a coat."

"What's wrong with the jacket? It's warm enough." He was wearing a lined black leather jacket that was more than enough most times and, once he adjusted to the temperature here, it would be fine. It was just quite a bit cooler than home and he needed to acclimate.

"Oh, honey, so good to see you." An older woman embraced

Erica before turning her attention on him. "And you must be Brock. I wish I could say I'd heard a lot about you, but it would be a lie. No matter. We'll get to know each other soon enough." He hadn't expected it, but the woman pulled *him* into a big hug, too.

He hated to admit that it made him feel warmer than the jacket.

Followed by her letting go, Erica's father pulled him into a hearty handshake. "Brock, very nice to meet the man who has captured my daughter's heart. My house is your house, as they say."

"Thank you, sir." Yes, it was definitely going to be difficult breaking her parents' hearts.

"Come in," her mother said, an arm back around Erica's shoulders. "I have hot cocoa ready to go. Only take five minutes to get you a mug."

They all walked up the stone path toward the house, with Erica's father pulling her luggage.

Once inside, Brock felt a tiny pang of...was that jealousy? He'd grown up in a large middle-class home complete with vaulted ceilings and art pieces he and his brothers weren't allowed to touch. Unlike it, this home was cozy and inviting, mirroring Erica's parents—which made him wonder a little about her. She was a lot of things, but she'd never felt *inviting*. For all he knew, though, she might have felt like she had to wear a mask to fit in with other lawyers—and that wasn't necessarily a bad stance. A fire burned brightly inside a stone frame, warming the entire living room.

"Let's take your coats," her father said, pausing inside the living room once they'd closed the door, shutting out the bitter cold.

Brock thanked the older man again. He appeared to be about his father's age, but this graying man had a head full of hair. Erica had the man's eyes, an earthy brown, shiny and a bit mischievous. He held his jacket while her father hung Erica's on a peg over a wooden bench.

"I'm going to get that hot cocoa going. Do you want any, honey?"

"Is the sky blue?"

Erica's mom chuckled and rolled her eyes before exiting toward the kitchen. In that woman's face, he could see all of Erica's other features—her high cheekbones and strong chin, her slender but short body, and her more-than-adequate breasts.

"Okay," said her father. "I'll show you to your rooms."

Hmm. Brock hadn't known exactly what to expect, but it didn't completely surprise him that Erica's parents were old-fashioned and, in spite of the phony engagement, put them in separate rooms—that was, if he understood Mr. Larson correctly. Brock knew his own parents would likely have them sharing a room—but he'd break that news to Erica later.

"Oh, I forgot to tell you that dad's name is Darren. Mom is Loretta."

In front of them, scaling the stairs, her father said, "Or you can call us mom and dad if that's more comfortable. We did that with our in-laws. Just seemed to fit somehow. But no pressure—you call us whatever you like." At the top of the stairs, her dad chuckled. "Just don't call me late to dinner.

"Erica, your room's in the same old place. Brock," he said, walking down the hall a little farther, "this is the guest room. Mama put fresh sheets on the bed today and a couple of blankets. We didn't know how you'd feel about the cold, so we gave you an extra quilt."

"We were just talking about that on the way over, dad. Turns out Brock's alma mater is Western."

Oh, this woman was going to blow their cover. "You'd think we would have talked about that already."

"Well, when you're in love, you don't always talk about rational subjects. And I'd imagine, with you two being lawyers, that you have lots of work-related things you like to discuss." Dad opened the door and flipped on the switch. "I'll let you both get settled in and then meet you down in the kitchen for cocoa." He started walking back toward the stairs. "I suppose I should have asked if you're even up for hot cocoa—or if you're just so tired, you want to hit the hay."

"It was a long drive, but I'd love to unwind and spend some time with you and mom before bed." Erica looked over at Brock. "What about you?" Seeing her in her old surroundings seemed to soften her features, and he didn't think she'd ever looked so lovely to him. Again, this was not good. But who was he kidding? The fact that he couldn't really have Erica made him want her all the more.

"Whatever *you* want, honey." Just in case she needed a

reminder that they were playing roles.

"Thank you, sweetheart."

Was there a bit of sarcasm in that?

"You kids," her father said, amused. "See you downstairs." Well, maybe it hadn't been sarcastic, because surely her dad would have picked up on it.

Erica went into her bedroom and Brock stepped into the guest room. There was a dresser against the wall and a closet to the right, but he didn't plan on unpacking. They'd be leaving sometime Friday and so taking everything out of the suitcase just to put it back in so soon after seemed like a complete waste of time. But he looked at the artwork on the walls—it was all something generic in the Thomas Kinkade vein of small town charm. But, he supposed, that matched the patchwork quilt on the bed and the look of unfinished log cabin walls in the bedroom instead of the traditional drywall. He knew that was the design of the house rather than reality, because he doubted those type of walls could retain heat.

He set his luggage on a chair by the window and then left the room, switching off the light. He walked the few feet to Erica's room and tapped on the open door. She was unpacking a couple of things and hanging them up. "Yeah?"

"You trying to give away our secret?"

"What do you mean?" Before Brock could answer, she said, "You mean the whole Western's your alma mater thing?"

"Yes."

"I think we're fine."

"Yeah, I do, too, but what about the next time when your mistake's not so easy to cover?"

"I'm sorry. I'm just a little tired."

He nodded and stepped one foot into the room. "So this is where you grew up?"

"Yeah. Mom and dad moved here when I was a sophomore in high school. We'd lived closer to the college before that."

"It's a nice place." He started looking around at the walls. There was a bulletin board above the dresser and there were photos of Erica and other people as well as what looked like an old high school football schedule and some other little things. There was also a bookshelf full of mostly paperbacks, and he couldn't help but smile when he saw that Perry Mason took up an entire row. His old bedroom? When he'd left his parents' home, he was pretty sure his mom had converted it into a pottery studio or some such bullshit. And that was fine, because he never intended to move back.

One of the photos on her bulletin board showed Erica hugging two young women who appeared to be close to her age at that time. "When was that picture taken?"

Erica closed the drawer and turned to see which one Brock was pointing to. "Oh, that's my cousin and one of my friends from high school." She walked over to the bed and pulled out a small bag before walking back to the dresser and adding, "I haven't seen her in a few years. She moved to Florida after she finished college."

"That seems a little extreme."

"She wanted to get out and never look back. A few of my friends were like that...but I've always loved my home."

Telling her about the real him would be dangerous—but he was going to do it anyway. Being honest with her might allow her to want to help him for more reasons than just moving up the ladder in the firm. "I was a lot like that. You want to get out of the nest and stretch—but when I got out, I realized maybe home hadn't been so bad."

"I don't think Carly will ever feel that way. We try to keep in touch, so we email each other every six months or so. She loves it there. I think she tries to come home for a few days every year, but she doesn't miss it."

"What about *you*?"

Erica took a deep breath and looked around her room as if trying to locate something deep inside. "Yes, I miss it, sometimes terribly. But I've built a life somewhere else and I'm giving it a go. I know home is always here if I need it."

"Seems like a healthy attitude."

She walked back to the bed and zipped up the suitcase before pulling it down and rolling it against the wall. "Ready?"

Brock couldn't resist the impulse to pull her close, because even though she still projected the strong, independent woman vibe, she had opened herself up a little, and underneath the shell, he saw innocence, sweetness, and maybe even a little vulnerability. He was pretty sure he liked everything about this woman. Lust? Yeah, in spades...but to actually *like* her as a person, value her as not just a woman but more...

That made her real.

That made her almost a friend.

Or more.

But he wasn't thinking about all that as he wrapped his arms around her waist and pulled her into his body. "So why the separate rooms? Don't most engaged people sleep together before marriage?"

Her glowering chocolate eyes made her sexy as hell, and the thought of friendship had already disappeared like a thick fog breaking up under the sun. "Nice try. Lucky for us, my parents have traditional ideas about what couples should and shouldn't do before marriage."

He wanted to get under her skin. Pressed against her, he remembered just how much he wanted her, and so there was no controlling himself. "Are you telling me you're a virgin, Erica? The good little daughter who waits for marriage?"

Her voice was barely audible when she hissed, "Don't be daft, Brock. My parents might like the appearance, but they're not stupid."

The smirk on his face couldn't be helped. "I just think our act would be more believable if we actually slept together."

Struggling out of his grip, she said, "Nice try, mister, but I wouldn't sleep with you even if you offered me your dad's position." She let out a huff and smoothed the form-fitting long-sleeved fuchsia t-shirt she'd worn for the trip. "Now...let's go spend some time with my parents—if you think you can behave yourself."

She would never admit it, but he knew he'd scored. He could tell she was thinking about having sex with him and that was a first step to actual conquest. Hoping his expression seemed mollified despite feeling like he'd won a victory, he nodded and held out his arm. "Lead the way, milady."

The only thing now was to keep himself from admiring the way she walked and looked in her snug blue jeans, because being a lusty guy would completely undermine the fiancé feeling, maybe having her parents calling their bluff—and he couldn't have that after working so damn hard to get here.

CHAPTER EIGHT

HOW HER MOTHER did it every year with no help at all amazed Erica, especially after the morning they'd had. She'd risen at seven so she could help her mother, because she knew the entire family would be coming for the meal, probably arriving around one o'clock. Before bed last night, mom had shown her all the pies she'd baked the day before—four pumpkin pies, one pecan, a lemon chiffon, two chocolate cream, and four cheesecakes.

Guess it helped having an entire week off from school and, unlike her father, mom had no papers to grade or class preparation for the following week—she had nothing but free time. When Erica had been growing up, though, her grandmother would have Thanksgiving at her house. Mom would make a dish or two and a couple of pies and then they would head to grandma's around ten so mom could help her put the finishing touches on the big meal, but since grandma had passed a few years ago, mom had taken up her mantle, and the entire Ruskin family—mom's relatives—continued gathering, just not at grandma's. Dad's family hailed from Grand Junction, and the family spent part of Christmas break and different times in the summer with them.

It wasn't just the love she felt for her mother and father that brought her home but also her love for their traditions. On this particular day, she would see family members that she hadn't seen in a year. Yes, they kept in touch through Facebook, but Erica knew that was a watered-down version of whatever her relatives were really going through, and it wasn't the same as having a conversation. She was nearly giddy with excitement, even when she learned that her brother and his wife and kids were going to be spending the day with her parents in Santa Fe.

By the time Erica joined her mom in the kitchen, the turkey was already in the roaster and mom was cutting vegetables for a huge lettuce salad. "What can I do, mom?"

"Help yourself to a little coffee first, honey."

Nodding, she noticed a big list written in Sharpie hanging on the refrigerator. *Ah.* So that was how mom did it. She had an agenda, a big to do list. After she poured coffee and doctored it with cream and sugar, she read through the laminated plan on the fridge. It was cute. There were big red Xs over the pie section, as well as the lines for turkey, Jello and cranberry salads, deviled eggs, and the relish tray. Next to the turkey, there was a line and mom had written *8:00* next to it. Erica knew that meant that either the turkey would be done by then (unlikely, because she could hardly even smell it yet) or—more likely—would need to be checked and basted.

"So do you just work off your list here?"

Erica could hear the smile in her mother's voice. "Yes. I finally got smart a couple of years ago. I used to write out a list the week before and then check everything off and, at the end of the day, I'd toss it, but now I have a permanent one. I have a shopping list on the computer that I print out every year, so now I don't forget anything. There's no going back for anything. I'm completely prepared. The list really helps."

"So just go down it and find something?" She glanced at the next item. "You want me to prep the ham?"

"No, I can do that, honey. What's after that?"

"It says *yams.*"

"Okay, then you can start peeling—and you can peel the white potatoes, too, while you're at it."

So Erica started working her little tail off, and she and her mother began chatting nonstop. When Brock got up an hour later, her mother offered him coffee.

"I'd love some, but I want to take a jog first. Do you mind if I have a glass of water?"

Erica tried not to smile because, in the short time she'd known Brock, he usually had a *bottle* of water—no ordinary plebian H_2O from the faucet would ever be good enough for this man.

"What? Drinking from the tap?"

"I think I remember the water here tasting good and cold straight from the tap—and a lot safer to drink than in the city."

As he walked to the sink, Erica noticed he was wearing a black Adidas velour jacket and athletic pants with white stripes. Sure, she'd known Brock was in amazing shape but didn't know he was into running—one of the most boring forms of exercise Erica could imagine.

"Darren's taking his walk before he settles in to watch football all day long. You might be able to catch him."

"I was thinking about running around campus—seeing if everything's the same since I left it."

"I'm sure it's beautiful right now, and the limbs of the trees probably still have snow on them from a few days ago."

"I know the sidewalks there will be clean enough for running. Plus I have an old route I used to run that starts at the library parking lot. I know where to run to get in one mile, two miles, or five, depending on my daily goals."

"This a serious thing with you?"

"I try to run every day. I feel better when I do."

"Well, you haven't lived at this elevation for a while, so be careful."

Brock smiled. "Thanks for the concern, Mrs. Larson, but I'll be okay."

"Please call me Loretta."

"Loretta." Brock set his now empty glass down next to the sink. "I'll see you after a while, honey," he said, kissing Erica on the temple. She was grateful he hadn't tried to get all handsy with her like he'd been doing around his own family, because her reaction would likely have given her away to the woman who knew her better than most.

"If you want some breakfast, I'm sure Darren will be in here when he gets back and he can make extra for you."

"Thanks. I'll be good till the big meal, though."

After he left, following her mom's directions, she checked on the ham and turkey, planning to baste both. Mom said, "He's a handsome fellow, honey."

In her mind, she was telling herself, *Think dreamy.*

Think sexy.

Ooh. The sexy part wasn't too hard, and she let her neurons grab onto that when she replied. "Yeah, he is, isn't he?"

"He seems to think the same about you."

Did he think she was sexy? That made her brain go places it really shouldn't.

She made sure her back was turned while she basted the turkey and gave her mom a not-quite-true answer. "Guess that's why we're getting married. We're compatible."

"So tell me how you met, honey, and what led you to deciding to marry so quickly."

Shit. This would involve a lot of lying (and she didn't like the idea of lying to her parents—the pretense was bad enough), and she'd also have to update Brock so their stories meshed.

Then again…adding some truth to it would help. "His brothers were the ones who interviewed me at the firm and subsequently hired me. I didn't really meet Brock until he was working late one night and so was I—and he invited me to have coffee with him." Mostly true. Choosing her words carefully, she could continue down that path. "We discovered we both had common goals—and it just kind of blossomed from there." Now for some distraction. "He spoils me, mom. Look at this ring."

Her mother paused from chopping celery to gaze at the diamonds on Erica's left finger. "I can't believe I didn't notice it before."

"And he moved me from a cubicle on the first floor to an office on the top with a view. I'm not stuck doing research anymore. I'm shadowing Brock right now, but the idea is I will soon be working with my own *real* clients with real cases."

"Good. I know you haven't been too happy with what they've had you doing."

"I'm excited now for the first time in a long time." And then she moved on to talking about some of the actual cases Brock was working on, careful not to breach any kind of confidentiality by not giving up details.

But the distractions only worked so long. Mom kept asking questions about her and Brock, and she'd have to give another little white lie before turning the conversation back to mom, asking questions about family members, her job, dad's job, what was going on in town, what their vacation plans were for next summer, etc., etc., etc. She thought she'd done an artful job keeping her mother off track.

Mom must have sensed something, though, because the questions kept coming.

What's your official wedding date, honey? Sometime in the spring. We haven't decided for sure yet.

When do you want to have kids? Oh, geez, mom. I have no idea.

He does want kids, doesn't he?

Gulp.

Well, sure, why wouldn't he?

So how many kids do you want? Gosh, mom, can't you just let us enjoy each other for a while before I start popping out kids? Besides, I need to relish my job first, don't you think?

Oh, of course, honey. I didn't mean anything by it. It's just that Jeff's finally started having children, and I think I love being a grandma. I know, mom. Sorry. I didn't mean to fly off the handle like that.

No, honey. It's okay. I'm sure you're getting questions like this from his family, too.

Only in her mind did Erica think that no, the questions just didn't have answers—meaning she and Brock probably had a lot more talking to do on the drive to Vail...because she didn't want to be this un-fucking-prepared again.

She hoped that, by Christmas, this whole charade would be over. Then she and her mother could have a calm, relaxing conversation again—and hopefully she could pull off a what-the-hell-had-I-been-thinking act.

Maybe she should have gone jogging with her fake fiancé to take some pressure off. Damn it all to hell. Hindsight really was 20/20.

In spite of feeling a little overwhelmed by the enormity of Erica's extended family and the gigantic feast her mother had put together (not to mention all the food the relatives brought along to supplement what was already there), Brock felt surrounded by a cocoon of love, happiness, and camaraderie. It was so different from his own family's gatherings. By the end of the meal, several of them, himself included, loaded dishes into the dishwasher together. Erica stationed herself at the sink to wash the pots and pans, and Loretta guided her helpers. Some were wrapping and covering up food while leaving it out for afternoon grazing, and a lot of the men were heading to the living room for an afternoon of football.

Aunt June, Loretta's sister, a heavyset woman with her shoulder-length hair dyed blonde, patted Brock on the shoulder. "Don't tell anyone, but Erica is my favorite niece, and I'm happy to see that she snagged such a handsome fella for her husband."

Brock turned on the charm. "I'm the lucky one, June. I assure you."

Her lovely brown eyes twinkled. "I think you both are."

"You brought the dinner rolls, right?"

"Yes—my mother's original recipe."

"They were the highlight of the meal."

June giggled like a school girl. "Don't tell Loretta that. The stuffing is supposed to be what everyone oohs and ahs over."

He winked. "It's our little secret."

"So, Brock, I don't know if anyone told you, but now you have two choices. A lot of the men—and my daughter Sidney— watch football the rest of the day like they hadn't seen it a game for years. The rest of us play board and card games in the dining room. It makes for a good time."

June's son Daniel, who appeared to be either a senior in high school or maybe even a college freshman, said, "*Three* choices, mom. Some of us head to the family room and either play videogames or nap. You know turkey makes me sleepy."

"You play football?"

"Yeah. Running back. I'm hoping to be a starter next year."

Which meant college. Damn. That was how Brock could tell he was getting older—it was harder to gauge a younger person's age. He nodded, hoping his face expressed to the young man that he was impressed. June kissed her son on the cheek and said, "So get to it, boy. I'm going to need you as my pinochle partner later."

"All right, ma."

After Daniel left, June said, "For now, handsome man, *you'll* be my partner in whatever we play."

"I take it we're in heavy competition?"

"Oh, yes. And you just joined the winning team."

How this woman had discerned his competitive streak was beyond him, but it was on.

And, throughout the laughter, the grazing, the joking and teasing, the winning and losing throughout the afternoon, Brock might not have fallen in love with Erica, but he had with her family...and, as he sipped a glass of egg nog later that evening, staring into the fire as a football game raged in the distance while people left one by one, his heart ached a little, remembering the real family, dysfunctions and all, he was going to be trying—and failing—to enjoy the next day.

It almost made him want to tell Erica they could spend the entire weekend in Gunnison...if he didn't think it would ruin his chances at inheriting his rightful place in his father's firm.

Maybe it was time to add some schnapps to the nog so he could sleep in peace later that evening.

After a few minutes, Erica sat next to him. "Thanks for being so good to my family."

Pulling his eyes from the flames in the fireplace, he said, "Are you kidding? It was easy. Your entire family is friendly and funny and welcoming." He took the last sip of his egg nog. "I wish I could say my family will be half as accommodating."

She was silent for a few moments before she said, "We come from different worlds; that's all."

He could hear Erica's mother and Aunt June, his game partner for a good chunk of the day, nearing them. He kept his voice low when he said, "Don't panic, but I'm going to put my arm around your shoulders."

Smiling, she said, "Fair enough."

Hmm. Why was this getting easier?

"*There* they are!" Aunt June's voice filled the living room, in spite of the football game's raucous sounds across the way. "We're leaving now if Danny'll get off that damn PlayStation."

Both Brock and Erica stood. June put her arms around Erica first, hugging her close. "It was so good seein' you, girl. You hang on to this handsome devil of yours," she said, winking at Brock. "I think he's a keeper."

"Thank you," Brock said as June moved to hug him and her daughter followed, wrapping her arms around Erica.

June said, "Our Erica is a special girl. I'm so glad she's found you."

How he was going to hate breaking all these people's hearts— way more than his own family's. *Way* more.

*   *   *

Brock's driving didn't seem nearly as scary the next day, even with all the mountainous roads they were sailing on. After a couple of hours, they were finally on the last stretch, heading up I-70 toward Vail, and the skies were clear. And although she'd had to cut her time with her family short, she could at least say it had been a great time.

"Hey," she said, and Brock tilted his head toward her. They'd been in another comfortable silence, and Erica still marveled at how it didn't bother them. "I wanted to thank you."

"For what?"

"Well, one, for warning me last night that you were going to put your arm around me. It was much easier to pretend then. And thanks too for being so good with my family."

"Like I told you, Erica, your family's easy to like. But now? Now we're going into a little bit of a different situation."

"Yeah…but life's what you make it, you know?"

She knew his family and, even though she was irritated that they'd squandered her skills for so long, she felt like her chances of being appreciated were a thousand times better now.

As they continued the ascent, barely noticeable even though they were speeding along the four-lane highway, just the way Brock seemed to like it, he said, "We're almost there."

"This is a beautiful drive. I've never been to Vail."

"What? Are you kidding?"

"No. I've been all over Colorado—my parents took me camping every summer, usually to someplace new every year—but we never came up here."

"I wonder why. This entire area is one of the most beautiful places in Colorado."

Erica started laughing. "If you have money."

Brock started to say something and then stopped himself. Probably a wise move. "Well, I think you're going to like it. I want to show you the creek and the clock tower—hell, the charm of the whole town. There's a bus that'll take us anywhere we want to go. I promise you'll love the natural beauty of it."

She had to get in a jab. "With or without the ski trails that have all the trees carved out?"

"I forgot you're not a skier. But it's beautiful anyway."

On that subject, they would have to agree to disagree. But,

because she'd never been here before, she really would have to reserve judgment until she saw it. And, so far, what she was seeing on the trip was absolutely beautiful. Of course, she'd always felt that, as long as she was in Colorado's mountains, she couldn't go wrong. Evergreen trees and aspens adorning a mountainside were her definition of awe-inspiring splendor, and man's creations couldn't touch what nature came up with.

One thing she *could* say if he asked was that she loved how the mountains hugged them on both sides, creating a narrow valley of green and white. And finally, through the trees, she could see, below and to the left, signs of the town beneath all the snow.

She had to admit, even if only to herself, that it really *was* gorgeous.

"You like?"

Damn him for reading her like a street sign. "Yes. It's pretty up here."

"I knew you would. I can't wait to show you everything I love about this place. And I think my whole family feels the same way—so if we get on each other's nerves, there are so many things about the village we can enjoy away from each other." He took a right onto an exit ramp and said, "And I promise—no turkey here unless that's what you want."

"I don't mind. It's only once a year."

"We'll have some dining experiences. Even though we're in a condo, my mom doesn't cook. She did some when I was little, but I barely remember it. We had a chef by the time I was in school."

Brock's mother seemed nice enough, but it made Erica wonder what the heck the woman did during the day if she didn't do things like cooking. And she was just assuming that, if his mom didn't cook, she didn't clean either.

As if he could read her thoughts, Brock said, "Mom ran several charities—still does, I think. She feels that donating your money and time is important for the betterment of mankind."

Okay, Erica could get behind that. "That's cool. What are some of her charities?"

"Hell, I couldn't tell you. She changes them all the time anyway. You can ask her later." Brock turned to the right and then said, "Don't expect to be impressed. There usually isn't anything in the bunch I'm familiar with but it's better than her cooking."

What a grim assessment of his mother. She could tell there was some sort of fracture in the family makeup—well, obviously, considering the sons were vying for a piece of the pie and their dad had some unorthodox expectations for what would make his sons good lawyers.

"I wish I could tell you what to expect, but it's different every time. I do need to warn you that it's a four-bedroom condo. I can sleep in the chair or on the floor, but I'd appreciate it if you could pretend like we're sleeping together, just so it seems believable."

Ah...he was asking. She was grateful for that—and she hoped her gracious reply would communicate as much. "Of course. Your family is the reason why we're doing this, so I understand it's important that they believe we're actually engaged."

"I might have to hug you on occasion, too."

Oh, of course. Just because it had hit her wrong, she added, "Would you like me to fake a loud orgasm while I'm at it?"

Brock was driving down a quiet road surrounded by evergreens. The valley was now shrouded in shadow, making Erica feel chilled to the bone. She was looking out of the passenger side window, but there was no mistaking the amused tone in his voice. "I wouldn't advise that, unless you really do want me pouncing on you for real."

The fact that he found it funny made her smile. She turned her face to him and said, "If a voyeur is a peeping Tom who gets his jollies from watching people, what is the audio version of that?"

"An audiophile? Is that it? Like a pedophile but a horny listener?"

Erica started laughing. "You perv."

"I'm not actually just into the sound. It's the overall package. You know, sight, sound, smell, touch." He pulled his car into a quiet driveway just off the road, right in front of a garage door.

"Taste."

He shut off the engine, enveloping them in sudden and complete silence.

"I do best when all my senses are stimulated."

She tried to keep her cool but she suddenly felt warm all over. "I think we can all say that. We all, uh, enjoy ourselves more when we're fully immersed." Gripping the door handle, she pulled it open.

"We should all be that fortunate to have that kind of lover."

In silence, they met at the trunk. Brock handed Erica her luggage and said, "Sorry. No warm welcome here like at your parents'."

"That's okay. It's cold out here. I'm sure they're just wanting to stay warm."

His dry tone said it all. "Oh, I'm sure that's it."

If Brock's family was half as bad as he'd been making it sound, she was going to be miserable this entire time. Erica was grateful they'd be leaving Sunday morning—first thing if she had any say in the matter.

CHAPTER NINE

HE'D TRIED TO warn her. And now she was sitting on the edge of that queen-size bed acting sad and forlorn—and there wasn't much he could do about it.

They'd walked inside the condo late in the afternoon. Elle and Bret were out doing something. Brandon, Lisa, and Saffy were eating dinner alone somewhere. His father was working on something (or at least that was what Brock's mother said)—so much for being a vacation—and she was already *snifting* the brandy, so to speak. The remnants of an argument hung in the air like a lead balloon, so Brock kissed his mom on the cheek and then peeked in the study and said *hello* to his father before showing Erica the way up the stairs.

"We should have stayed with *your* family, eh?"

Erica was a trooper—Brock could appreciate that much. "It's all right. Maybe I'll just go to bed, if it's all right with you."

"No. No, it's not. You haven't eaten since your tiny salad at Mario's. We'll walk through the village, hop on the bus, and we'll have dinner some place. Everything will be decorated for Christmas and covered in snow. I promise you'll love it."

Oh…maybe he was overselling it. He didn't want Erica to know that if anything brought out the boy in him, it was the town of Vail. Yes, she was right in that it was a rich kid kind of place, but as a child, he hadn't known that. He'd loved the cool, quiet summers there and the beginning of ski season—all the Christmas lights in town glittering against the snow.

83

Although Erica arched a beautiful eyebrow, she paused, considering his words. "I guess that's what your fiancée would do, isn't it?"

"*My* fiancée? Hell, yes."

She nodded, and he didn't even care that the way her shoulders slumped communicated reluctance. "All right. Let me just change clothes."

"What's wrong with what you're wearing?"

"I want something warmer—a sweater and boots." She held up a hand, fingers splayed. "Five minutes."

While it was a good idea that she be warm, he was itching to get out of the condo—no matter that they'd just arrived. The atmosphere was oppressive, negative...stifling. Somehow, it felt just a little more bearable with Erica in tow—but he wanted to save her from it, keep her happy. She was pure bliss to be around, even as feisty as she'd get, when she was enjoying herself. He hated seeing her reflection of the general mood of this place.

They'd have enough to battle tomorrow. Tonight was theirs.

A real fiancée would change her clothes in front of him with no qualms—but she wasn't a real bride-to-be. And, much as he wanted to tell her how they'd follow through with his ruse, she was helping him, so he wanted her to have some say in the matter. "Do you want me to turn around or wait for you downstairs?"

"You can just turn around while I put on this sweater," she said, pulling a burgundy one out of her suitcase. "We don't want to give them a reason to be suspicious, right?"

He nodded and smiled, glad they were on the same page. He turned around and looked in the direction of the television. When they talked strategy over the next day, they'd have to turn it on. He didn't think his parents would eavesdrop, but he'd put nothing past his brothers. Its noise should easily drown out a quiet conversation.

Looking around, he noticed there was no furniture other than a wooden chair and desk. He supposed he'd be sleeping on the floor for two nights...unless he could talk Erica into sharing the bed.

"Okay, I'm ready."

But first he had to help her fall in love with Vail. She loved her hometown Gunnison, so Vail should be easy.

They bounded down the stairs and Brock said in the general

direction of his parents, "I've got the keycard. We're going out for dinner. Be back later."

He heard his mother say, "I think Brandon and Lisa are at—" but he closed the door quickly enough that he could honestly say he missed it. There would be no fucking running into his brother. They'd have to deal with him soon enough. For now, it was just him and Erica.

Out of instinct, he was sure, Erica walked to the passenger side of his car, but he came up behind her, placing his hand on her back, and said, "Not taking the car. We have just a little way to walk to where the bus will pick us up." He began to lead her in the right direction, his hand still on her back, and asked, "You okay with walking?"

"Yeah, that's okay."

"Do you jog?"

Erica laughed. "Not if I can help it."

She wasn't throwing his hand off, so he left it there. In case any family members saw them, they'd be convincing. "Well, if you decide to give it a try, there are some nice places to run here. I love jogging along the creek when I can."

"I don't mind walking."

"Then maybe tomorrow morning I can slow down my jog and we can walk to Starbucks."

Even in the dusk, he could see her eyes light up—or maybe he was just imagining it. "You're on."

"In the meantime, I'm going to take you to one of my favorite restaurants here."

"What is it?"

"You'll just have to wait. But what I like about this place is they're really into serving local organic food. Ever eaten elk at a restaurant?"

"What? Seriously?"

"Yeah."

"No, I haven't eaten elk at a restaurant—but I don't think I want to."

"If they still have it on the menu, I recommend it."

"That's okay."

"Fine. Will you have a bite of mine if I get it?"

He could hear her sigh, but he could also see her breath rushing out in front of her, thanks to the cold air surrounding them. "All right. But please tell me they have some kind of chocolate for dessert."

"They should. Want me to check their menu on my phone?"

"No, that's okay."

"Right up there—see?" He pointed to where he knew the bus would be stopping, and as if it arrived solely by his thought, he heard it close. "Shit. Are you up to running?"

"You really want me on the jogging bandwagon, don't you?"

He laughed. "No, but if we don't hurry, we'll have to wait for the next bus." He wasn't going to divulge to her that another one would probably arrive in twenty minutes, even if she felt warm. The restaurant wasn't too far away if they needed to walk, but the bus was truly the way to go. "Race ya." There wasn't any snow on the sidewalk, so he wasn't worried about sprinting in the dark. He glanced behind himself and saw that she wasn't in any big hurry. "Come on, Erica. The bus'll be here any second." Facing her, he continued running backward.

"Shit, Brock. You're going to hurt yourself!" She started running then—at a decent clip even—and caught up with him. Once she caught up, he turned, grabbing her hand, and they raced the rest of the way together, just as the bus stopped and opened its doors for three people already standing and waiting.

By the time the two of them boarded the bus, they were laughing. Finding a seat near the front, they sat down and he said, "See? You never know when that kind of training is going to come in handy."

She shook her head. "You're crazy."

The lights on the bus dimmed. After a few seconds, he saw that she, too, was looking out the windshield. "See? Christmas lights and trees everywhere. Like the North Pole, eh?"

Erica nodded and smiled but just kept looking. The driver stopped the bus again, letting on two people while the majority of the passengers that had already been onboard got off. "It *is* pretty," she said.

"Yeah. I knew you'd think so."

And either she hadn't noticed or she didn't care that his arm was around her shoulders…but he wasn't removing it unless she told him to, because something about her seemed more like family than his own flesh and blood, and he was beginning to think he didn't want to lose that feeling.

* * *

Dammit. Erica was way out of her element and she even felt underdressed, but she wasn't going to complain. The creek side restaurant was indeed beautiful...but it felt way too high class for her. While she'd never felt inferior to wealthy people, she'd also never been comfortable around displays of luxury and riches—and this certainly was one. Yes, sure, they were serving "common" elk and trout on the menu, but those entrees didn't come out on the plate like her mom would have made. The food here wasn't what she was accustomed to. If, for instance, it wasn't served with a demi glace, it had a reduction or a vinaigrette—and appearance was key, which was probably why all the servings of meat seemed to have little bunches of greens on top. The only time that happened in Erica's world was when she ordered a cheeseburger and they put lettuce and tomato on it. And the portions here seemed skimpy. But she and Brock had an appetizer and some amazing wine to go with the meal, and she was feeling warm and just shy of giddy, in spite of being a fish out of water.

When the waiter came by, he asked, "Can I interest you in some dessert?"

Brock said, "I believe the lady would love something with chocolate."

"I have just the thing. And for you, sir?"

He looked at Erica. "Want to share dessert?"

Oh, did he look devilishly handsome right now. She'd share almost anything with that man at this moment. "As long as it's chocolate, you bet."

Brock raised an eyebrow at the waiter, who nodded his head and whisked away to fetch it.

"It's too bad we're here in the winter."

"Actually, we're not, Brock. It's still fall till next month."

"You know what I mean. The snow's on the ground—feels like winter to me. But I'd love to take you to the Alpine Gardens. It's a shame we won't be together next summer or I would."

Erica frowned, because he was almost making it sound like they were really engaged.

"But there's a really cool skiing museum in town. If it's open tomorrow, I could take you there."

She couldn't help the scowl still plastered on her face. "Shouldn't we be spending time with your family while we're here?"

"You tellin' me you're not sick of them already?"

Forcing a smile as the waiter approached them, she said, "I don't see them nearly as much as you do."

The waiter set the plate between them on the table, and it was indeed chocolatey. It looked like a brownie with caramel and chocolate drizzled over it, topped with whipped cream, much like how the mountains here were covered in snow. Erica began salivating as her eyes caressed it.

"Enjoy."

"It's a lot easier to avoid blowing our cover if we're not in the condo."

She dug her fork into the side of the dessert, loading it up with a healthy amount of gooey chocolate goodness. "True, Brock, but I feel completely out of sorts here. The bus was the closest thing that felt normal to me, but even that couldn't compare because it was free. I'm a stranger in a strange land here—in culture shock. Yes, the surroundings are lovely, but I still don't get how felling dozens of trees so rich people can glide down a cold mountain trumps the beauty of nature unscathed. We're deep in the Rockies, but there's no sense of roughing it."

"You're not *supposed* to be roughing it in Vail."

She sighed and closed her mouth over the fork. She shut her eyes, letting her taste buds take in the sensation of being jolted by chocolate and sugar. Mmm. It was amazing and helped her forget for five short seconds how she really did feel like the trout that had been on Brock's plate—not just a fish out of water but completely fucked as well.

Swallowing, she opened her eyes to see Brock tasting the dessert. "Yeah, that's obvious."

"What can I do to make you feel better about being here?"

If he'd been having a good time, she would have felt guilty about ruining it, but even though he loved the town, she knew he was miserable thanks to his family. What was saddest was they hadn't seen anyone other than his parents today and that hardly even counted.

At least they'd both be miserable. Sunday couldn't come soon enough.

* * *

"Trust me. After a good night's sleep, you'll see this place in a whole new light." Part of Brock wished he could understand how she felt, but he'd grown up this way. Nothing about the town or what Erica perceived as its wealth had ever bothered him, but it was getting under her skin. Maybe she misunderstood.

But, as they walked toward the bus stop in the chill dark evening, he thought maybe he could see things a little through her eyes. Unlike, say, east Colfax Avenue, there was no hint of poverty or even struggle here—meaning she was right about one thing: Wealth kept this town going—so if the good citizens wanted a Starbucks latte, by God, they got one.

She was missing the bigger picture, though, and it was that they were surrounded by natural beauty. Fine, if she hated looking at the slopes, she could look at the mountains on the other side of I-70, the ones where man had only built homes and roads but the majority of trees stood tall and proud.

It inspired him. "Do you mind walking part of the way?"

"No, that's fine by me."

He led her down by the creek where they could walk toward the condos but along the creek trail. Again, man had tended the area to sculpture nature's touch, but there was no denying the sound of the creek couldn't be enhanced or destroyed by anything the architects here could do. There were trees and dirt and rocks and dormant plant life, and the creek flowed. It wasn't so cold that it was iced over, so the babbling sounds were soothing.

He hoped she felt the same way. "Step carefully. The light's not that great here."

"The moonlight helps." After a second, she added, "I think you knew exactly what I needed."

The air was brisk and the snow beside the trail glowed brightly under the rays of the moon. The only sound Brock could hear was the creek, and he imagined it was as soothing to Erica as it was to him. Erica wandered off the path a bit to get closer to the creek. When she slipped a minute later, Brock reached out and pulled her up, close into his arms. Before he let her go, her body pressed into his, he said, "Maybe we'd better head back to the sidewalks."

"Yeah, I guess."

As they walked in silence until they were back in the village proper, with their hands in pockets to protect their fingers from the freezing air, he asked, "Did you get enough to eat?"

"I didn't think I would when I saw the tiny portions, but I'm pleasantly full. Not too much, though."

"Good. And we'll exercise off any extra calories in the morning."

"You're hell bent on getting me to run, aren't you?"

"Brisk walking would be fine." Brock's pace slowed. "Why don't we wait for the bus here?" While he felt like the few minutes alongside the creek had been good for Erica, he was ready to get indoors—and he figured she might be even more so, especially because the boots she wore looked like they were more for fashion's sake rather than warmth. But what did he know about women's clothing?

As the bus pulled up, he said, "We just need to make it through the next twenty-four hours. That's all. Then we're home free."

"Maybe you've forgotten about Christmas."

"Well…if the ink's dry on the papers dad will draw up soon, we won't have to worry about that."

But he had the sinking feeling that Erica might be right—and he wasn't sure how she'd feel about that.

Only time would tell.

As Erica and Brock approached the house, she was beginning to realize something—something she'd never admit to Brock.

The charms of Vail were beginning to get to her.

She despised money. She hated sensing that its influence was all around her—and not just pocket change. There was serious wealth around her, and she was most certainly going to stick out like a sore thumb. Maybe as long as they mostly stayed in the condo tomorrow, she'd fare okay. Even though she didn't feel at home with Brock's family, she felt comfortable enough—and if they kept the conversations centered around topics she was familiar with, she would survive.

This is temporary, she continued to tell herself, much like a cheerleader on the sidelines tells her team they've got that winning basket—even when they clearly don't.

But Vail was a gorgeous place, and she'd find it in herself to settle in until they left on Sunday.

By the time they got to the condo, Erica's nose was cold and she knew it would be pink or even red by now. Brock held the front door open for her. As she walked in, she hadn't known what to expect, but it certainly wasn't the sounds that assaulted her in the doorway.

"Damn it all to hell, Bret. You get to choose every year. It's *my* turn."

Erica recognized Brandon's voice and wondered to herself, *Does he know he sounds like he's two years old instead of a guy who's in his thirties?* She thought some of simply running up the stairs to their room, but Brock was unzipping his jacket, so she began unbuttoning her coat.

Bret's voice met their ears. "I really don't care, Bran. I just want to get the decision made. It really doesn't matter if you're the one who's making it. It just needs to get done *now*, because if you wait till tomorrow, it'll probably be too late to make a reservation. In fact, we should have already been done with this."

"I'm doing that now."

As Brock and Erica entered the living room from the entryway, they saw Brandon storming toward the kitchenette area. Lisa was on the floor playing with the baby and Elle sat in the large cream-colored sofa, sipping an amber drink without ice. Harper was still seated at the desk in the corner, working on something, and their father was nowhere to be seen.

"Hey, everybody," Brock said. "What are we doing tonight?"

Elle lifted her perfectly manicured eyebrows before saying, "I'm going to finish this drink and then retire to bed." Erica thought it odd that she was going to bed early, but the woman said, "I'm going to need to start getting my rest if I'll be carrying Bret's child."

Lisa said, "Yeah, enjoy it. Once your baby is moving, you'll be on her schedule."

Harper looked up from the desk, pulling her reading glasses down her nose, probably so that she looked more authoritative. "Lisa, I've told you that you can't let the baby dominate your schedule. It should be the other way around. You need to train her to adapt to your needs."

The younger woman frowned and muttered, "Yeah." Then she started looking on the coffee table past the stack of large glossy magazines. "Anybody see the TV remote?"

Brock cleared his throat. "Erica and I are going to be heading to bed ourselves, but I wanted to ask what time the big meal is tomorrow."

Bret popped out of the kitchen. "All depends on when Brandon can get the reservation for. Might be lunch. Dunno. Do you have plans we need to work around?"

"This is Erica's first time in Vail. I just wanted to show her around town."

Erica couldn't help but catch the hint of derision in Elle's voice. "Really? I thought everyone had been here."

"Erica's not a skier. She grew up close to Crested Butte, so there's nothing exciting about it for her."

Bret clicked his tongue. "Well, if she's going to be part of this family, she might want to learn."

Erica could feel her face flush. *I'm right here!* They were discussing her as if she was in another room, and it was beginning to frustrate her.

"We'll be skiing tomorrow if you want to join us," he continued, this time looking at her, almost as if he'd gotten a psychic message from her. "Our insurance is good if that's what you're worried about."

She didn't know that she was *worried* about anything, and she wasn't sure how to respond to his statement. Brock jumped in and rescued her, though. "One day isn't enough to really enjoy yourself, and Erica didn't bring any equipment or clothes or anything. We'll have to do it sometime later in the season when we have a couple of days, but, like I said before, I'll be showing her around tomorrow, not down the slopes."

"Suit yourself."

"I guess I'll check in with you in the morning—unless you want to send me a text." Brock placed his hand on the small of Erica's back, guiding her out of the room. "Good night, everybody." Erica followed up with her own *good night* before they rushed up the stairs. She didn't mind Brock's hand because he was saving her, whether he realized it or not. It might not have seemed like a big deal to Brock, but the atmosphere downstairs had felt toxic.

God, how could he handle so much dysfunction?

Once they were behind the closed door of the bedroom, Erica pulled off her coat and said, "Is it always that much fun?"

"That was nothin'." Brock peeled off his leather jacket, draping it on the wooden chair by the desk. "Can I ask you a favor?"

"Like I haven't already given you plenty?"

Brock smiled, charming as ever. "I didn't realize there wouldn't be much furniture in here. And I know I agreed to sleep on the floor, but that carpet is *not* beckoning me." He drew in a deep breath before asking, "Would you be all right if I slept on one side of the bed—on top of the covers and fully clothed, if that makes it easier?"

Erica might not have been a Brock fan, but she wasn't heartless. And, seeing the stock he came from, she was beginning to sympathize. That he turned out almost close to normal was saying something.

"Yeah, sure."

"You're a doll." Brock sat on the edge of the bed, pulling off his shoes. "In the meantime, do you want to see if there's a good movie on television? Unless, of course, you'd like to watch the trash Lisa does. I'm sure she's watching reruns of *Jersey Shore* or *The Kardashians* if you'd rather."

Erica laughed. "No, I'm good." She leaned over her suitcase, pulling out the things she'd need to get ready for bed—toothpaste and toothbrush; cleanser, toner, and moisturizer; lotion; pjs, robe, and slippers. Before she headed out the door to use the restroom to change, she turned to Brock. "I can say this much: out of your entire family, I think I have the most in common with you."

"I'm going to take that as a compliment."

Grinning, she added, "And, if it won't go to your head, I think I like you better than all the rest, too."

"You better. We're engaged, after all."

She rolled her eyes and left the room, thinking they couldn't end *that* soon enough.

Holy shit, was he in trouble. Erica returned from the bathroom wearing a fluffy black robe and matching slippers—

nothing exciting. But when she peeled off the robe, he spied out of the corner of his eye—although he pretended to be watching the Tom Cruise sci-fi movie on the television—a long, filmy nightgown in lilac. Even though it swayed against her form, his peripheral vision was able to make out the curves of her breasts and hips.

Not good. He was going to have to keep his hands and eyes to himself in this bed.

While she was gone, he'd taken the liberty of changing his own clothes. He'd taken off what he'd been wearing—sweater and jeans—and traded them for gray sweatpants and a white t-shirt and socks. Normally, he'd sleep either in underwear or nothing, but he'd promised to be dressed over the covers, so he had to find something halfway comfortable in his luggage. And while this getup might be too hot underneath a comforter, it should keep him warm on top of the bedding.

She held her phone in front of her face for over ten minutes, and he finally said, "You must have the most interesting Facebook feed of anyone on the planet."

Laughing, she replied but kept her eyes on the phone. "No, I have a Kindle app. I haven't really read much in the past year, but now I have a little free time. I have like forty or fifty ebooks on here that I bought a long time ago when I graduated and thought I might have some time for leisure reading."

"So what *are* you reading?" He imagined Erica to be the type to read nonfiction.

She almost giggled but he could see that she suppressed the impulse. However, she said, "None of your business."

"Aw. You can't say that to your fiancé and expect him to ignore it." She rolled her eyes but it didn't stop him from leaning in her direction and peeking at her phone.

"You can't tell what it is anyway."

"The way you're acting, I'd think it's the Communist Manifesto or something."

"Not quite."

He studied her face as she resumed reading—and then he realized that her cheeks had actually been pink.

"Hmm. Are you embarrassed about what you're reading?"

"Why would you say that?"

"Because you were blushing."

She sighed. "Here. You're so curious, why don't you read a little?"

He took her little Android phone and looked at the screen. At the bottom of the app, it said she was 64% of the way through the book, but that didn't mean anything to him. All he knew was she appeared to be in the middle of a chapter.

He started reading in silence.

He did that a lot, and I wasn't sure why or how he was able to tune me out. He sat on the couch, and so I was able to walk in and sit next to him. He was absorbed, and so I decided to kiss his neck, get his attention. But that's when I noticed what he was doing. He had up some Yellow Pages-type listing, and he had an entire page of people named Richards.

"Looking for family?"

As though he were pulled into the moment, he slammed the lid of the laptop down. "Nothing you need to worry about."

I was taken aback. "I was just asking." He set the laptop on the floor and kissed me with a hunger…or a vengeance. I'm not sure which. And he started unbuttoning my jeans. "Not here, Ethan."

"Oh…this seems a little naughty, Erica."

"Just give me back my phone, please, Brock."

"A little bit more…" He returned his eyes to the phone, swiping the screen to turn the virtual page. This time, he read aloud.

"No one's here right now, Val."

"I don't care. They could be back at any minute. I really don't want them walking in if we're in the middle of making love."

"Oh, is that what we're calling it? Making love?" I just looked at him and then stood up. "Don't you like it when I fuck you?"

"Sounds like a bit of a dysfunctional couple. But I want to see what happens next." He loved that he was getting under her skin—and it turned out he was right. The book was definitely a little naughty. He flipped the page until he found paydirt.

He read with a bit of a theatrical flair, as if he had a book of Shakespeare in front of him and he had to pour all his emotion into the words to help his audience appreciate the literature. He read it slowly, while trying to keep his voice sounding innocent for better effect.

In the short time I'd even been sexual, he'd figured out what buttons to push. Kissing my neck always made me melt and there went the anger. *And his hands went straight to the button on my jeans again. I was at a melting point and wanted to insist we go to my room, but I was so hot at that moment, I did just want him to fuck me. So I too was clawing at the button on his pants and not worrying that we still stood in the hallway just inches shy of my room.*

"Brock, stop."

"Stop *what?* Getting you all excited with words?"

"Just—" He let her snatch the phone out of his hand. "Let me read my damn book in peace, please."

"This is some of that so-called Mommy Porn, yeah? And what's the point, Erica?"

She turned on him, her pupils dilated so large he could hardly see her brown irises as her nostrils flared. "It's a *love story*, Brock, and it was sweet until *you* started reading it."

"Well, if that's sweet, I want some of that." He sat up, enjoying the hell out of getting a rise out of her. "What's the name of that book anyway?"

"Fuck you."

"Wow. Strong words coming from a lady like you." He scooted closer to her on the bed. "Unless you meant literally…and I could definitely oblige."

"Don't be a pig, Brock. I'm supposed to be in love with you, but it will be hard to act like I do when you're so repulsive."

"*Repulsive?* Wow. I don't think I've ever been called *that* before."

Erica slammed her phone down on the nightstand. "I am going to sleep now, Mr. Ford. If your manners have not returned by the morning, all bets are off. I don't care if I have to find my own way home."

"Fine. I was just teasing." Sensitive little thing.

"No more. This is serious business. I can't pretend to be your fiancée if you're constantly screwing around."

"Okay, fine. My lips are sealed."

"Thank you."

With a huff, Erica rolled over, yanking on the comforter, but it wasn't budging because of Brock's weight. He decided to wait so she'd have to ask politely before he got up to give her some slack in the covers.

In the meanwhile, he had some contemplating to do, because—in the words of Shakespeare—he was pretty sure she *doth protest too much.*

CHAPTER TEN

IN SPITE OF being a bit of an ass the day before, Brock acted the next morning as though nothing had happened. He insisted on getting Erica out of the condo before ten, though, and they took a brisk walk through the town, pausing at Starbucks before resuming.

In the middle of their journey, Brock got a text from Brandon that they would be having dinner, not lunch, so Brock used that as an excuse to be gone most of the day. He took Erica all through town, telling her about different memories he associated with various places.

The sky was a light blue with few clouds, sunny and bright, and Erica asked, "Does it snow here much?"

Brock looked around, particularly toward the ski area. "Hmm. What do you think?"

"Very funny. I *know* they get a lot of snow, but it's been clear the whole time we've been here."

"It's in the forecast for tomorrow afternoon, the main reason why I want to leave early tomorrow."

Erica wouldn't be hard pressed to admit that she enjoyed her time with Brock that day. He was lighthearted and playful, a quality that Erica never saw him display around family or at the office. In fact, he'd been that way the night before when he'd been embarrassing the hell out of her reading from the romance book she'd been devouring. When she'd handed over her phone, she had just finished reading a sex scene, so she'd thought she was safe. Leave it to Brock to find more, though...

But he hadn't said another word about it the next day and he'd since been lively and fun. If the real Brock were like this all the time, she'd have no issues playing his fiancée. It was his asshole moments that made it difficult.

When it was time to head back to the condo, Brock estimated that they were about a mile away. "Race you."

"You'll win."

"Come on, Erica. It's the perfect temperature for running— not too cold and the sun is shining on us. You're wearing sneakers and you finished your bottle of water. Come on. It'll be fun."

So she ran part of the way, but she grew tired after what she estimated was half a mile. Brock told her that they'd only gone one quarter.

"Well, I'll walk the rest of the way. Meet you there." She could tell he was itching to run. "Seriously. I can find my way back. Go."

"Nah. I can walk with you."

"Would you just go already? I'll be fine." She thought some of telling him that all the rich white people residing here had created the perfect crime-free neighborhood by ensuring no one without money or needs of any kind could live there, but keeping those kinds of negative thoughts in her head would sour her mood again.

But at least he took the hint.

As Erica walked alone, she took in the natural beauty of the place. She loved the snow, the mountains, the clear sky as a backdrop, and she focused on those things. The beauty of nature—that was what brought her joy more than anything manmade, and it was those moments she'd need to hold onto during dinner with the dysfunctional Ford family, because that was sure to be a treat.

Brock tried to keep his cool. Erica hadn't brought any formal wear on the trip, and they hadn't shopped for it while they'd been out and about all day, but when he mentioned it later that afternoon, Elle said she might have something Erica could borrow. Elle was the taller of the two but her tea-length dress nearly touched the floor when Erica wore it. The dress, a deep shade of jade, made Erica's brown eyes all the more vibrant.

Lisa had a pair of black heels that fit Erica's feet so well, Cinderella's prince would have been fooled.

When Erica walked down the stairs so they could go to the restaurant, Brock felt a lump in his throat. She was stunning, just like she'd been the night of his dad's party. This woman really would look good on his arm permanently.

What the hell was he thinking?

They took two cars, and he and Erica rode with Brandon, Lisa, and the baby, a car seat separating Brock from his date.

That was okay, though, because she was on his arm when they entered the restaurant. As they were walking in, she confessed to him that she wasn't always comfortable with these sorts of places and he said, "Yeah, they're not my favorite, either, but sometimes you find a chef who makes it all worth it." As they approached the table, he put his lips to her ear and said, "This is the kind of place Brandon loves—all pomp and circumstance. But this is what we came for—and, after this, we're under no obligation for anything else the rest of the time we're here."

Erica's gracefulness in the restaurant as he held her chair for her to sit belied her inner toughness. Brock was truly beginning to appreciate how elastic Erica could be—professional one minute, the doting daughter the next, and now, a truly elegant woman.

His father needed to hurry up and finalize his plans, because Brock didn't know how long he'd be able to play loving husband-to-be without giving in to those strange emotions.

It was a dangerous game he was playing.

He hoped Erica wouldn't feel out of her league here, considering what she'd had to say last night. This place was more upscale than where the two of them had dined the night before. Linen napkins and tablecloths and at least ten utensils at each place setting.

Ah, well, this was probably the last shindig she'd have to attend like this with him. She'd live. And she'd probably like the food here, in spite of how she felt.

They weren't seated for long before his family began their usual bullshit. Brandon was quiet and sulking while Lisa tried to cheer him up with the baby. Bret was also acting typically sycophantic, trying to smooth things over with his parents while ingratiating himself, and Elle was already perusing the wine menu.

And his mother and father were the ones causing all the waves, seeming to be completely oblivious to it all.

Of course, Bret and Brandon were in a pissing contest, not unlike ones he'd seen many a time, trying to one up each other.

As usual, he was being ignored. At times like this, he was fine with that.

But the trouble was brewing.

"I just wish you'd looked at the menu before reserving a table here, Brandon. You know Elle is gluten sensitive, and they don't seem to give a damn about food allergies here."

"That's not true, Bret. Just because they haven't indicated anything on the menu doesn't mean they're not willing to accommodate." Brandon was acting like he was perusing the menu, but Brock could tell he was actually trying to find something on there to shut his brother up. "Besides, you knew I've been wanting to go here for years. If you didn't want to eat here, you could have made the reservations yourself."

"You agreed to do it."

"That's enough," said father Ford. He snapped his fingers and their waiter appeared almost out of nowhere. It was a hell of a talent, Brock thought, and definitely a dying art. "My daughter-in-law can't eat gluten. Do you have anything gluten free?"

"I can ask the chef."

Elle, her voice low, said, "I'm fine."

"But honey—"

"I'm *fine*." The waiter was already gone when Elle added, "I'll just have a little gastric distress for a while, but that's okay. I need to purge a few pounds anyway."

Jesus. These idiots were making a horrible impression on Erica. He glanced over at her and saw that she'd buried her head in her menu, scouring it as if she'd never eaten in a restaurant before.

Minutes later, the waiter was leaning over the table, pointing with his pen at menu items that Elle could eat that the head chef had indicated were gluten free. "The chef also said that he can convert some of the menu items to be gluten free, so if there's something you'd prefer, we can put in a request."

"No, that's okay. I think I'll have the quinoa and vegetables dish."

"Perfect. So are we all ready to order then?"

The ordering process, followed by the big deal the waiter made over the bottle of wine and serving it, which was quickly followed by their appetizers, made everyone at the table focus on food and fun rather than petty bickering.

But that didn't mean Brock couldn't feel the undercurrent. It was coming.

Even *he* felt like giving Elle shit, though, because the appetizer—mini egg rolls with a variety of sauces—probably had gluten, and that hadn't stopped her from eating a couple without even asking the waiter.

Lisa didn't feel like holding back, though. "Elle, I'd be careful if I were you. I think the egg roll wrappers probably have gluten."

Elle cocked her head and, even though her voice sounded as sweet as honey, there was no mistaking the venom behind it. "I'm pretty sure they use rice flour for these."

"Well, what about all the dipping sauces? They might be thickened with flour...and I just thought you'd want to be careful."

Ice couldn't have been colder. "Ever hear of cornstarch?"

Erica must have been getting stressed by the ridiculous amount of tension, because she blurted out, "They are definitely delicious—hard to resist!"

Everyone seemed to pick up on the hint, because they all then began talking about how good the food tasted, focusing on that instead of one person's dining habits. Then, when it got quiet at their table, Erica turned to speak directly to his father who was sitting at a diagonal from her. "Sir, since I'm going to be part of this family soon, I thought I should ask you if there are any Thanksgiving traditions with the Fords that I should be aware of."

Brock's father blinked twice while swallowing the last little bit of egg roll in his mouth. Then he looked down at the table as if contemplating before he answered. "You know, Erica, I can't think of anything in particular that we do, aside from what we're doing right now. We spend the weekend here in Vail and always have our Thanksgiving meal on Saturday. Why do you ask?"

"Well...my Aunt June has this cool tradition at her house—it was an idea she got from some movie she watched a long time ago, but I love it a lot and thought that Brock and I might want to do it with our family once we have children."

"What is it, dear?" his mother prodded.

"Well, my Aunt June has a white pillar candle on her table—

she calls it the Fire of Gratitude. Before dinner is served, she lights it, and before there is any eating, each person takes the candle and says something that they appreciate about one of the people at the table. They can mention more than one person if they like, and they're encouraged to say something nice about everyone—but that's not required. The idea is to inspire a feeling of gratitude through everyone before eating the Thanksgiving meal. She says it's to make us feel like we're supposed to on this special day."

"I think I quite like that idea," his father said. "We don't have a candle like that one, but we can do something like that right now."

Elle arched an eyebrow. "Maybe Erica can show us how it's done."

Brock was proud of her, because she didn't miss a beat, even though he could sense the snark behind Elle's suggestion. "Sure."

His father said, "Well, I'm sure she might be hard-pressed to say something nice about *all* of us. She hardly knows us."

"I'd be happy to try." Erica picked up the tiny candle in glass on their table and said, "Here goes." She turned to Brock. "I guess you're first." She inhaled deeply before looking Brock square in the eye and making him believe that she either truly felt the way she did or she deserved an Oscar. He realized it was all artful acting but, damn, she was good. "Brock, thank you for loving me, for asking me to be your wife. Thank you for giving of your soul selflessly, for trusting me, for realizing my true potential and nurturing it. I will forever be grateful to you for that."

Brock didn't have to act to beam from ear to ear—but he *did* have to stop himself from kissing her. Then she looked past Brock to Brandon. "Brandon, thank you for having enough faith in me to hire me at the firm. I hope to always make you happy with that decision. Lisa," she said, looking at the woman who thought she was going to be her sister-in-law in the near future, "thank you and Elle," she glanced across the table briefly, "for your generous spirits by letting me borrow your clothing tonight. And thank you for accepting me as your sister. Saffy, you make me smile. Keep being your cute little self!

"Bret, thank you for being a boss who's fair although demanding. Thank you for your faith in me and for letting me begin working with Brock. And, last but not least, to my future mother- and father-in-law, thank you for doing such a fine job

103

raising your sons. Brock is a good man, and any woman would be proud to marry him. I credit you with making him the strong, sweet man I fell in love with. And thank you all for accepting me into your family with open arms. I'm grateful to be here, and my future looks so bright now, thanks to you."

Well, no one at the table would be able to top Erica's performance, but he might as well try. She was waiting for someone to take the candle from her when the waiter came by to pick up appetizer dishes. The eldest Ford said, "Ask the chef to hold our food for a few minutes longer until we finish what we're doing." Then he turned his attention to the table. "Who's next?"

Brock already had the candle in hand.

"I'll go next, dad." He went around the table, trying to pick out a positive attribute of each person there—and it was crazy, because even though these people drove him completely nuts and he could probably go the rest of his life without dealing with a good lot of them, they all had qualities he appreciated or admired. Even loved. Like Bret—the guy might have been a bit obsequious nowadays in terms of their father and the business, but he was still sharp—one of the smartest guys Brock knew...which was probably why his behavior in terms of their father was so annoying. And Brandon—although there was no sign of it today, even a year ago, the man had been a natural comedian. He had a great sense of humor and an unusual way of looking at the world. Having a baby and a social climbing wife had kind of snuffed all that out, but during this gratitude exercise, Brock began to believe that maybe those qualities were just dormant.

His parents? Well...despite the fact that they could have been better, there were all kinds of good things he could say about them: as a child, he'd never wanted for anything. After college, he had a job waiting for him—and his education was paid for, too, and he knew that was a huge deal.

The women, Lisa and Elle? Well, he didn't know much about them—very little that he liked anyway—but he tried to see them through his brothers' eyes. Elle? She was model beautiful, a sight for sore eyes. And her fashion sense was spot on...at least that was what all his previous dates had told him. One thing he knew for sure—she could wear a dress like no other. Lisa, on the other hand, seemed to be a good mother. Yes, she relied on her nanny a little too much and seemed overly indulgent, but there was no mistaking that she loved her child and wanted the best for her.

Wow. After finishing, he almost remarked that it had been a lot easier than he'd thought. Instead, he held the candle out to the next person.

By the time everyone was done, he was more than ready to eat…but everyone seemed to be in great spirits, the best he'd ever seen at their traditional Thanksgiving dinner out.

His father finished, giving a long speech, telling his sons with sincerity how very much he loved them and how proud he was to be their dad. Brock imagined that, had he been a lot more sensitive, he might have teared up at the sentiment. It was good enough that he believed it wholeheartedly, and when his dad said, "Okay, let's eat!" everyone enthusiastically agreed. Smiles remained pasted on faces and dinner conversation was more enjoyable than he could remember—in recent memory anyway.

When they left, hearts and bellies full to capacity, Brock held Erica's coat so she could slip it on and, from behind, he bent over and whispered in her ear. "What you did tonight was nothing short of a miracle. I don't think I've ever seen my family so happy—or grateful. Thank you for that."

As she buttoned her coat and they began a slow walk toward the front while waiting for the rest of the family, she had a funny look on her face. She leaned forward and Brock got closer, sensing that what she wanted to say was for his ears only. "You have to promise not to tell my secret."

"Okay…but I'd say you're definitely one up on me. That makes you safe."

Smiling, she whispered, "My Aunt June doesn't really do that at her house on Thanksgiving."

"She doesn't?"

"Nope, but it worked, didn't it?"

"Hell, yes." And maybe, during the remainder of their little charade together, she'd manage to teach him a few more things about life—because, truth or not, that had worked. Brock could honestly say he didn't hate his family members…and he hadn't felt that way in a very, very long time, a feeling he was sure they could reciprocate.

And that made him all the more thankful for this woman, his pretend fiancée.

CHAPTER ELEVEN

ERICA HADN'T SEEN it, that little piece of black ice beside Brandon's SUV. Once she took the tumble in those ridiculously high heels, she spotted it from a different point of view.

From eye level, as it were.

It had happened so fast, just as she was getting ready to enter after the baby had been secured in the car, and after, the other three adults were hovering over her, asking her if she was all right. "I think I'm fine, pride aside."

"What happened?" Brock asked, holding her arm to help her up.

"Ice—just a tiny bit of it."

"That's all it takes. Does anything hurt?"

"I don't think so. And I think your shoes are okay, too, Lisa."

"Oh, I don't care about the shoes, honey. I can always buy more. Are *you* okay? That's what matters."

Her candle trick had worked. Lisa had never been this kind to her, not that she'd ever been mean—but apathetic to her before, yes. Now Lisa was actually acting genuinely concerned. And that made Erica want to not think of it as a trick. It was an exercise, and it had made this family more human again. She hoped they would continue it for every Thanksgiving from here on out.

For now, though, she said, "I think so. My butt and right wrist hurt, but I think I'm all right."

Brock was holding on to her, probably trying to make sure she wouldn't fall again—and he didn't leave her side until she was buckling herself in.

As they drove back to the condo, part of her wished it would snow, because the air always felt magical when the flakes were floating down from the sky—but inclement weather would make for a shitty drive back to Denver tomorrow, so the rest of her was glad there was no precipitation.

When they got to the condo and she got out, she felt a stiffness in her back. Brock joined her on her side of the car and asked, "Are you *sure* you're all right?"

"I'm not going to have you pressing charges against the restaurant, Brock. I'm fine."

They started walking toward the door, just a few steps from where Brandon had parked in the garage, and once inside, entering the kitchen, Brock said, "I'm not a sue happy lawyer, Erica."

"Aren't you the tort king at the firm?"

Bret, fetching ice out of the fridge, said, "He might not be king, but I don't know what we'd do without him." He lowered his voice and added, a teasing note to his voice, "Besides, his specialty really is criminal law. He just takes the occasional tort for fun."

"Fair enough. And, while falling in the parking lot was unpleasant, I don't think it was criminal."

"You fell? What happened?"

Erica gave Bret a short account of how she'd hurt herself and, by the time she was done, Elle had joined them. "It started out with my butt and wrist hurting, and now my butt feels better, but my back has kind of locked up."

Elle said, with a purr in her voice, "Oh, you should have Brock give you a backrub. He gives the best massages."

Erica paused, glancing from Elle to Brock who had one of his typical smirks on his face, then over to Bret, who seemed completely oblivious to the fact that his wife had just implied that Brock's hands on her body had felt better than anyone else's.

Creepy.

"No, I'm okay. I'm just going to lie down and hopefully feel better in the morning."

"You want an ice pack maybe or—?" Brock asked.

"Maybe an ibuprofen or two."

"You got it. I'll bring them up."

So Erica headed up the stairs, glad the eldest Fords weren't in the living room so she wouldn't have to explain what had happened again. She decided to change out of the dress and shoes first, because she wanted to feel comfortable. Before, though, she locked the door in case Brock decided to come in first.

She wasn't changing into the gown this time, though, because Brock seemed to like it way too much. Instead, she had a t-shirt and sweat pants, and those would look a lot less appealing. She was pulling the pants up her leg when he knocked on the door. "Erica, it's me."

"Just a sec."

Damn. Yeah, the more time passed, the more her back ached. She made her way to the door and unlocked it. Brock handed her a couple of rust-colored tablets and a glass of water. Once she swallowed the pain reliever, she said, "Can you give those black pumps to Lisa, please? And, if you could, let Elle know I'll have her dress laundered and get it back to her when it's done."

"Sure will." He started to turn but paused. "Do you need help getting into bed?"

"I'm not an invalid, Brock."

Smiling, he said, "I didn't say you were. I just want to help if you need it."

He was right. He was being generous and kind, something that didn't seem to come naturally to him. "Thank you, Brock. I mean it."

"No problem." He left the room and she took her time heading back to the bed before pulling the covers down and sitting. Every breath seemed to highlight the pain in her spine, so she gladly lay down to take some pressure off. It still hurt, but it was definitely better.

Brock came in the room a few minutes later. She was trying to go to sleep, knowing her back would probably feel significantly improved in the morning, but the ibuprofen hadn't kicked in yet. "Can I get you anything?"

"No, thank you."

"Want to watch anything on TV?"

"No, not really."

Brock sat on the edge of the bed. "I'm going to make another offer to do a backrub. You never know. It might help."

"Yeah, or it might make it a thousand times worse. I'm afraid to have you touch it."

"How about you give it a try? And if it hurts or makes it

worse, I'll stop. Sound good?"

Erica still hesitated, nervous that his touch could make healing more difficult, but then she decided she liked the idea of being able to tell him to stop if it got to be too much.

She just had to be sure to not think about him doing it to Bret's wife—and Elle somehow finding it erotic.

"Okay, so how do we do this?"

"Lie down on your stomach. Make yourself comfortable. I'll straddle you, okay?"

Still dubious, she said, "Okay," and rolled over. She positioned her arms underneath the pillow and moved around, trying not to hurt her back.

"Ready?"

"Mmm-hmm."

In a few seconds, Brock climbed on the bed and, true to his word, straddled her upper thighs. "Can you tell me where it hurts?"

"On the right side, just above my butt."

She felt a slight brush on that area. "Here?"

"Yes." She tried not to be snappy.

"All right. I'll avoid that area. It seems like if you can relax the muscles around the sore ones, your whole back feels better before you know it." He adjusted a little and said, "So just relax."

Closing her eyes, she tried. At first, her muscles were tense, probably with fear that he was going to hurt the hell out of her, but after a while, she was able to experience the magic that was Brock's hands. He was finding lumps in her back she didn't even know existed, leaving the flesh left behind feeling melty and warm.

Man, she never wanted it to end.

And then, later, just as she was getting drowsy, he asked, "Feeling okay?"

She muttered an affirmative into the pillow.

"All right. Hold on, okay?"

In a moment, he was back on the bed, straddling her, but this time he was positioned higher, so that his crotch was cradling her ass. At first, she was a little alarmed, but she chilled again. "I got some lotion. I think you're almost asleep, so this should get you there." She expected a cold shock, but he'd warmed it up before applying it to her back. This time, he was gentler, applying sensual pressure, gliding over her skin in a way that was soothing...but hotter than hell.

Oh, shit. This wasn't good. Not good at all.

She had to make herself relax once more, this time because her filthy mind was going places it shouldn't. If his hands felt that good on her back, what would they feel like on the rest of her body? If he was that attentive with her when she was in pain, how much more so as a lover?

Holy hell. She was in deep shit.

And not surprised at all when she awoke the next morning in a light sheen of sweat, having dreamed of gorgeous Brock Ford fucking the shit out of her.

Monday morning, Brock was in the office before seven AM. After being off work for several days, he wanted to beat most of them there so he could have a little quiet time and get a handle on his day.

But at eight o'clock on the dot, Erica entered his office, rapping with force on the door. He looked up from the case he'd been perusing to see her standing there with a serious look on her face. Her hair was pulled up, not in a bun but up off her neck so that she looked professional. Her jewelry was understated...but that wasn't what caught his eye. She was wearing a dark blue suit that hugged her curves and heels that added so many inches, she was probably close to his height—but he hadn't stood up to find out.

Before he could even offer a *good morning*, she asked, "What's on the agenda today?" He started to come up with an answer but she continued, "When do I get to take a case?"

He swallowed. Damn...she was firm and heated. When he'd dropped her off at her apartment the night before, carrying her luggage upstairs so as not to restrain her back, it had taken everything in him to not pull her into his arms and kiss her like there was no tomorrow. And, unfortunately, here at work he most certainly couldn't get away with it.

Before they officially "broke up," he would have to have her...just one time.

For now, though, he had to play employer.

"Well, why don't we look over the clients we're going to meet with today and you can pick one?"

He saw a bit of shock registered on her face, as though she hadn't expected his agreement to come that easily. But he saw no reason to fight her. She was smart and capable and only needed the chance to prove herself. Half of being a lawyer in the courtroom was being a good actor, and he already knew she had that down pat.

"Umm, okay. When do you want me to come back?"

"You don't need to. I'm ready to prepare for appointments. First one's at eight-thirty, so we need to get started." The emails, preparing for tomorrow's hearing, all that stuff—it could wait until later. "I have more appointments than usual today. Having a few days off makes Monday a little busier." Erica sat in one of the client chairs across from him on the other side of the desk. "Why don't you bring one of those chairs over here so you can look at the computer screen and case files with me?"

"Okay."

It took everything he had to not stare at her ass in that dress as she pulled the chair around. And he already knew what those shoes would make her calves look like. Shit…he had to get his mind out of the gutter and concentrate.

"All right. So we've been inundated with more clients than we can handle right now. By all rights, I should have been working over the weekend."

"You did. I saw you answering emails on your phone."

"Yeah, I should have been doing more, though…but I wanted a bit of a break. That's part of why we were hiring a while back. We foresaw the need for more attorneys on staff, but the problem, as you already know, is we're so buried that we're using and abusing you guys to do the work we just can't get to and we're not really getting around to training you like we should."

Her smile was sweet. "Well, you are *now*."

"Yes, but to the point—I'm not handling the kind of cases I prefer or even ones in my expertise. They're all over the place, so if you want to take lead on a couple of them, no problem. I can guide you but let you do the work and decide within reason how to handle it."

"Really?" She acted like she almost didn't believe him.

"Yes." He grabbed a thin manila folder off the stack. These particular folders were currently thin because they hadn't filed any motions yet. All they had were a few brief notes taken by paralegals in initial non-billable (read: *free*) consultations. But that was enough for him and Erica to go on before they met with the clients to get an idea of what they would be discussing.

He handed her the folder. "Typically, you'll get something like this from one of us. Dad, Bret, Brandon, and I will take the cases we either want or need and pass on the ones to the associates we think will do best with them or who seem to be handling their caseloads just fine. But, like I said, because we've been swimming in work, especially since May, we're getting bombarded. It's best for a client to meet with the attorney assigned to the case, so we try to shuffle them off before this first meeting if we decide not to keep them, because the client will have a hard time thinking of someone else as 'their' lawyer. I'd planned to keep all these, just because I don't have anyone to give them to. Everyone's overworked here right now, but these seem pretty cut and dry, so I should be able to work them in my sleep."

Erica's smile flashed like a Nikon. "You can give them to *me*."

"I intend to give you one or two. Once I know you're on the right track, I'll give you more."

"Two cases won't be enough to keep me busy."

"I'll have you helping with mine." When she nodded, he pointed to the file in her hands. "Go ahead and review the notes and tell me the kinds of questions you think we should be asking." When she opened the folder, he peeked at it momentarily to refresh what he already knew. If he recalled, it was a sexual harassment case, but the details seemed vague. He wouldn't say anything to Erica about it, but he'd gladly let her take that one. While he felt like their firm could be a good champion of equality and fairness in the workplace, he didn't think he was the attorney to handle it.

Erica began jotting a few notes and he turned to his computer to sort through a few more emails.

"Okay, so here's what I think." Brock took his hands off the keyboard to give Erica his undivided attention. "I think we need to ask her what happened—or, more precisely, give us a timeline of occurrences. Like…what events have transpired? Has she talked to HR at her place of employment?"

"Yeah, sure, those are good questions. More often than not, though, you're going to ask her to talk and that will lead to organic questions. What I did when I was fresh out of school was make sure I was familiar with the particular laws surrounding what my client was visiting me for."

"So...Civil Rights Act?"

"Yes. If we have time, we'll pull up the statutes, kind of skim them a little to make sure we know exactly what we're dealing with. There are also some pertinent state statutes surrounding sexual harassment." He picked up his coffee cup and saw that he'd drained it minutes ago. If he had a chance before the clients started filing in, he'd grab one. "Next."

"But—"

"Erica, we have twenty-five minutes if we're lucky. You're going to need to make decisions quickly before we start looking at laws. Because once the clients start coming in, we need to give them our attention. Every minute with them counts—literally."

She batted her eyelashes, looking a little irritated, but she clamped her jaw and picked up the next file. Based on his own history, he knew what that clenched jaw meant—she was biting her tongue to refrain from saying anything that might cause friction. She opened the folder and skimmed the notes quickly. Ah, she already had the right idea. "Okay. This woman says her employer has forced her to work untold hours without compensation—clocking out early while actually continuing to work, that kind of thing." Before he could even ask, she rattled off, "Federal and state labor laws, especially FLSA."

Nice. "Good. What next?"

"Which is the one coming in this afternoon?"

"It doesn't matter. If these clients take too long with us, there won't be another chance to review. We prep now."

"Okay." She clenched her teeth again...and why the hell did he find her so damned cute when she did that? But she once more breezed through the file before setting it down. "Racial discrimination on the job. Another civil rights suit." She looked up, not even asking if it sounded good to him, and set the file on top of the others. Picking up one of the last files, she said, "I thought you preferred criminal work."

Brock couldn't help the smirk on his face, because, as he recalled, he thought there was one there that was closer to it.

Less than a minute later, she said, "The client this time is a defendant. He's accused of sharing trade secrets with the public and, therefore, rival companies…and his defense isn't that he didn't do it, but that the trade secrets were nothing of the sort."

"Go on."

"He was apparently blogging on the side, trying to make money by sharing all the crap that made him hate his job—and the employer is alleging that a good portion of what he shared isn't his *to* share. We have a copy of the complaint, and it says that the workers are required to read the employee manual and sign off that they have done so."

"Law?"

"This still feels kind of like civil rights."

"Yes, but we're on the defense side now, so we need to think a little differently. We might also want to look at the possibility of a plea agreement. Sometimes we can negotiate with the plaintiff to see if they'd like to accept a lower penalty to our client in favor of avoiding a costly lawsuit that, frankly, I could find a way to drag out for months."

"Why would you want to do that?"

"Lots of reasons—it gives me more time to prepare but it also weakens the other party. If they're just wanting to be done with it, the longer you stall, the more likely they will be to settle for something less. But this? Why didn't they just demand he take that shit down and then fire his ass or write him up or something? And maybe they have and this was a last resort. So…you might think case is more like to the kind of case I prefer, but no. If you don't want it, I'll slough it off on another associate."

"No, I'll take it. I'll take whatever you give me."

"Okay. I'm not particularly interested in *any* of these today. I'd prefer—"

Brock's secretary, a middle-aged woman with light blonde hair and tired gray eyes, peeked her head in the door. "I'm sorry, Mr. Ford. I have one more."

"That's fine, Harriet." He took the case file from her. "When are they coming in?"

"Squeezed them in at ten."

"All right." He handed the file to Erica as his secretary left. "How long has she worked for you?"

"For me personally?" Erica nodded. "Since I started here—so about six years."

"And you still make her call you *Mr. Ford*?"

Brock couldn't help but chuckle. "I do no such thing. She's been here at the firm for close to twenty years. It's her thing. I don't mind being called my first name by employees, but I'm not going to beg her to do it. The one time I told her she could call me *Brock*, she seemed shocked. Probably because my dad insists on being called Mr. Ford and won't answer people if they call him by his first name. Well, I guess I should clarify—here at *work*, he views everyone as a subordinate and demands that they all show respect...and one way they do that is how they address him." He nodded at the fresh case in her hands, one he hadn't seen yet. "So what have we got?"

He glanced over to skim the document as well, but he didn't finish it by the time Erica began talking. "Another civil suit. This time a young woman—looks like she's a college freshman—is suing for the right to use the men's locker room whenever she pleases."

"What?" Surely, he hadn't heard correctly.

But Erica confirmed. "Yeah. Not just during practices or games or anything specific. She just wants access and, of course, the college denied it."

Brock rested his forehead on the tips of his fingers for a moment. "Where do these people come from?"

"I don't know...but I guess we're representing her in her fight for justice."

"She's lost her fucking mind—but, I suppose, she must have been willing to pay the retainer."

Erica just nodded but jotted a couple of notes. "So which of these cases do you want?"

"None, frankly. But I have to admit I think you already have me figured out. If I had to take one, it would be the blogger one." He sat up. "Instead, you need to tell me which ones you'd like to represent—how about two for now?"

"Two? Are you kidding?"

"I'm trying to go easy on you."

Erica let out a sarcastic half laugh. "You guys had me doing research for months on end—usually twelve to fourteen hours a day—and now you want to *go easy*? That's rich."

"In all fairness, Erica, that was my brother, not me."

She blinked a couple of times, slowly inhaling, before she said, "You're complicit. You're one of the brothers set to take over the firm."

He arched an eyebrow. *Damn, she was feisty today.* *Normally, he loved it, but right now she was poking a tender spot.* "Look...right now, I'm the low man on the totem pole. Say I'm complicit if you wish, but know that I really can't tell my brothers what to do. Even when we take over, I can't imagine being able to boss them around."

"But you can tell them if you see an injustice."

"Maybe in the future. Now? No. That's not my place."

She acted like she was going to say something else and then thought better of it. She finally said, voice sweet as honey, "Can I take all five cases? At least you'll only have to consult on them."

*Truth be told, he couldn't find a reason not to let her. People learned better by doing, and she already had all the education she'd need. From this point forward—especially *because* she'd no doubt become quite adept at research—she'd become better by actually practicing law.*

Rolling his chair back a little from his desk, as if conceding a point, he said, "Okay. They're all yours."

"Really?" She giggled, a behavior that seemed a little incongruous considering the professional air and clothing she wore, and then spontaneously leaned over and kissed him on the cheek.

Brock, normally confident, mostly good at reading signals from women, was stumped. Should he take that little peck on the cheek as something or blow it off?

For now, because she got right back to business, he was going to disregard it—but that didn't mean it wasn't floating around in his mind, teasing him...just below the surface.

CHAPTER TWELVE

ERICA COULDN'T BELIEVE her score, landing so many cases just starting out. She credited the fact that she looked the role. Thank the heavens her back was feeling all better, or she wouldn't have been able to wear those ridiculously high pumps.

"So," she said, looking at her fake fiancé, trying to pretend she hadn't just kissed him on the cheek. What the hell had she been thinking? "We're going to look up statutes now?"

"I'd rather grab a quick cup of coffee, because we might not have another chance until this afternoon."

"Seriously?"

"All depends on how fast we get through each interview. And, honestly, they're the ones paying, so they can stay as long as they like."

"Okay. Then I'll get some, too."

She expected them to go to the tiny kitchen where they'd first met, but she found out there was a coffee pot upstairs as well. Erica was wondering why when they first met he hadn't just gotten coffee there instead of downstairs, but his secretary cleared it up for her. When they approached the pot in the conference room, Harriet said, "Fresh pot's made, boss." He thanked her and poured a cup, and Erica realized that he didn't make the coffee— he had his secretary do it. She might have to talk to him about that sometime.

But she wasn't really upset about it—not right now, anyway. Her head wasn't where it should be and she was struggling with it.

She should have been contemplating her future clients—all five of them—and thinking of questions to pose, strategies to consider, arguments to make; instead, her brain was stuck on Brock. When she'd impulsively kissed him, she'd gotten a whiff of his spicy cologne. It was his trademark, and after sharing a bed for two days and the close confines of a car several times over the past weekend, she realized she loved the scent.

And she was seriously falling for him.

He was a gentleman when he wanted to be, but even his rougher edges appealed to her.

What the hell was going on inside her head?

She shook her head when she heard him repeat her name. "What?"

"Hold out your mug."

She'd been holding her hands down at her sides, the coffee cup dangling from her right fingers, but Brock was going to pour her some. "Thank you." If only he knew what she'd been thinking...

Think about the clients, *Erica.* The bottom line was that she considered herself a people person. She had no problems talking to folks, asking them questions, letting her intuition guide her. How difficult could it be to gather information for a potential lawsuit? She could wing it, no problem. On their way back to Brock's office, she said, "I think I'm ready for our first client. I have a couple of opening questions."

"I think it would be better if you let me do the first few and then you can do the rest."

Oh, she was tired of his bullheadedness. "Why? You'll be right here. If I mess something up, you can step in." He got ready to say something more, so she continued. "If I need more information, what's going to stop me from contacting them later? You act like it's such a big deal."

"Goddamn, woman. You are stubborn."

Erica's shoulders dropped. "Sorry." She was just excited, but she didn't know that she'd be able to explain that.

"But you have spunk. I love that, and it will serve our clients well."

"So does that mean—"

"No. First interview's mine. But maybe I'll let you do the rest."

He'd called *her* stubborn? But he'd still acquiesced some, so she was going to take his offer. "Deal."

Erica had gotten through the first three client interviews just fine. Brock had been a little overbearing at times, not letting her follow her own instincts when it came to questions. Instead, he'd interject what he felt was important to the case. During her first interview, she simply bit her tongue and let him take over but took back the reins as soon as he'd let her.

By the second interview, she felt her anger start to rise and, by the third, she was ready to explode, and so, during their quick lunch of a sandwich and chips Harriet had picked up for them, she tamped down her emotions and calmly told Brock she felt like she was ready to handle the next interview completely by herself.

While he'd said that was fine, it seemed like he was blowing her off, because he wasn't giving her his attention. Instead, he was checking and responding to emails between bites of food.

She'd harrumphed and flipped open one of the case files. After they were done with interviews, they could discuss strategy, but what was the point? She had the feeling Brock was going to simply tell her she needed to file this motion and that, contact so-and-so's attorney, etc. She was pretty sure he wasn't going to let her come up with her own ideas first.

"Sorry, Erica," he said, as she continued looking at the file, "but this is the kind of life you're going to have to get used to. When I'm on the clock, so to speak, I'm working. You might have gotten your ideas about attorneys from TV, but it's not the life of glamour Hollywood makes it out to be. When you're spending time with clients, you're not doing the actual work, and when you're doing the actual work, the inquiries don't stop—emails and voicemails, phone calls, and sometimes drop ins. Harriet picks up as much of that for me as she can, but there's only so much she can do, and there are a lot of questions she can't answer—either because they're questions seeking legal advice or they're things she doesn't know the answer to. I just want you to know that if you think life will be easier here than when you were doing research, you're wrong."

It was like he didn't know a thing about her. "I didn't think that. I *want* to work hard. This is the part I'm passionate about."

He looked at her then, eyebrows raised, an expression almost conveying surprise. "Okay." The desk phone rang and Brock hit a tiny button on its face. "Yes?"

"Your next appointment is here."

"We need about five minutes, Harriet. I'll call you when we're ready." He looked over at Erica. "Did you get enough to eat?"

"I'm fine."

"Okay. Let's clean up in here. If you need to go to the ladies' room or anything, now's the time."

"Nope, I'm good. I have all my questions prepared." That way maybe he wouldn't feel the need to derail her—or, if he did, she could get back on track. As requested, Erica crumpled up the trash from lunch and tossed it in the wastebasket under Brock's desk. "I still have soda in my cup—should I set it somewhere else?"

"You're human, Erica. You can have a drink here unless you're prone to spilling. And we always have water and coffee for the clients if they get thirsty." Without warning, he dialed Harriet; in seconds, she responded, and Brock asked her to show the client in.

Harriet arrived, looking a little less tired than earlier in the morning, and said, "This is Kylie English." Both Brock and Erica stood to shake their new client's hand and Harriet left as they all sat down.

Kylie looked to be thirty-something and she was a tall drink of water. She was also thin with red hair, a smattering of freckles on her nose and cheeks, and bright green eyes, almost the color of a blade of grass. She slapped on a huge smile, but somehow Erica could tell it wasn't completely genuine—and she knew it had to do with why she was here—sexual harassment.

"Kylie, I'm Brock and this is Erica. I'm a senior partner here at the firm and Erica is an associate. She'll be handling your case but I'll be overseeing it—and that's why we're both here today."

Why Brock couldn't let her handle the introductions, she had no clue. He'd made a big deal out of Erica needing to be the person they associated with their case, so he needed to shut the hell up. But Kylie was the last case of the day, so she was just going to let that go. She only hoped the clients would have confidence in her abilities—in spite of the fact that it seemed like she needed a babysitter.

"Nice to meet you, Kylie," Erica said, shaking the woman's hand. "Please have a seat." All three took their respective chairs and then Erica said, "I've reviewed the interview you had with the paralegal last week, but would you mind telling me more details about what happened to you?"

"Yes. Thank God. I wanted to tell that girl last week and she told me to save it for you after I only told her one thing."

"Do you mind if I take notes?"

"Not at all."

"Begin whenever you're ready."

The woman pulled out a small red notebook and flipped to the first page. "My dad always told me to document things at work when they got weird...and, man, did they get weird." She was scanning through her notes and said, "Before I tell you that stuff, I need to, I guess, disclose something. So I work at Pioneer Manufacturing. I've been there for about eight years. I started out on the assembly floor—boring work but it paid the bills. There were dozens of us in the warehouse, and employees came and went like there was a revolving door out front. Anyway, after the first six months, I got a promotion into the QA Department. I was thrilled. Even though I didn't like the idea of being a cop, I liked that I would be making more money and not stuck doing the same thing all day long.

"I wasn't in QA long before my boss and I started dating." Erica paused from taking notes and looked up at Kylie, raising her eyebrows. "No, *he* wasn't harassing me. The attraction was mutual. But we didn't work out—and, when we didn't, I started looking for another department to transfer to. I didn't care much for the job in QA anyway, but then having to see my ex every day made it a little painful. It just so happened that the shipping department had an opening, and I was lucky enough to get a job there.

"So, because I'd never been in that part of the plant before, I had no idea what to expect. Yes, I'd gone to the foreman's office for an interview the week before, but I hadn't actually gone deep inside. Our lockers there weren't like the ones in assembly or QA." She shook her head as if to emphasize her point. "I need to back up a second and tell you that shipping, for some reason, only had men working there. It's not like the job is hard—I mean, sure, sometimes there's some heavy lifting, but most of it's done with pallets and a forklift. And it's definitely no more dangerous than assembly. But, for some reason, women avoid that part of the plant like the plague. Pioneer tends to employ more men than women anyway, but shipping is literally a No Woman's Land—until me. And that's okay. I didn't mind. Sometimes I prefer working with men because they're not as catty as women can be." She smiled then—this time, a genuine one—and said specifically to Erica, "Sorry. No offense."

Erica smiled back. "None taken." That little exchange made her feel as if she was starting to build a little rapport with her client, and that was a good thing.

"Anyway…the locker rooms. Each guy had—on the *outside* of his locker, mind you—a pin up poster of a naked girl. Wasn't that a thing a long time ago—naked girls pinned up in overtly masculine places, like auto shops and stuff? Not that it matters. I felt like I'd entered another country. It was so weird. And if they'd had them *in* their lockers, even that wouldn't have been so bad. I could have ignored them then.

"So I started wondering if it was stuff like that that put off women from working there. But I thought, *Hey, I'm the new kid. I gotta pay my dues,* and I didn't say squat about it. It made me uncomfortable, especially a couple of extremely nasty pictures that kind of made my skin crawl."

Brock interrupted, "Did you say anything to you supervisor?"

"Not then. I just figured I'd deal with it. Some pictures? Okay, no biggie. I just wouldn't look at them when I went to my locker, which was, like, three times a day, five max. I've been in uncomfortable work situations before, and it seems like if you ignore stuff like that, it eventually goes away."

"But these guys? They were disgusting pigs." She looked at Brock. "No offense." He just shrugged and shook his head to indicate to their client that he was all right. "They'd tell really filthy jokes around me all the time and, at first, I just tried to ignore it—kind of like the locker room, you know? But it got to a point where I couldn't tolerate it anymore, because it was like they were escalating. *We didn't get a rise out of Kylie that time. Maybe this'll work.*"

"So why didn't you think you should say something to them or your supervisor?"

Erica could tell Kylie was making her way toward that and

why Brock was hounding her, she couldn't say, but he wasn't letting her lead. She gave him a glance, her eyebrow raised, hoping he'd take the hint.

"Well, I finally *did* say something to the guys. One of them, a guy named Dale, was telling some stupid disgusting vampire joke about a woman on her period, and that was the final straw for me. I mean, here we are, busting our butts, packaging this huge special order for one of our best clients in Texas, and they're screwing off playing comedians. I stopped what I was doing, made sure I was loud enough to be heard by them all, and said, 'Excuse me. I'm flattered that you think I'm just one of the guys, but what you're saying is kind of offensive.' Instead of apologies, I got responses like, 'Well, sorreeeee!' and 'Aw, do you wanna go back to the kitchen now?' Just really rude stuff."

"Sounds kind of like they were egging them on," Erica said.

Before Kylie could answer, Brock said, "You don't want to lead our client."

Erica could have died. Okay, so maybe to a degree, Brock was right, but it wasn't like Kylie was on the stand in court. "I'm just trying to get a sense of what was happening."

Instead of replying to Erica, he said to Kylie, "Please continue, Ms. English."

Erica could keep her cool, but she was starting to get pissed.

"For the rest of the week after that, they were all pretty quiet, you know? I thought they were trying to respect my wishes, and I was glad I'd said something, you know, stood up for myself, even though those guys were kind of intimidating.

"But then, the next week, it was worse. They kept talking about 'this woman,' saying stuff like, 'One time there was this woman. She thought she was kinda smart but she was actually kind of stupid. Anyway, one day she tells her old man to shut the fuck up. An' know what? He pops her, square in the jaw. Taught her to keep her mouth shut.' Seriously. They talked like this all day long nonstop. Finally, I said, 'Guys, I know what you're doing. Very funny.' And they'd say, 'What, Kylie? Why does shit always have to be about you? Careful. Your head's gonna get so big, it won't fit through the door'."

Brock said, "Our paralegals said you documented these behaviors? Days, times, people?"

"Yes."

Once more, Erica had to bite her tongue. Yes, it was all there in the file. Why did he feel the need to interrupt her story?

"So, throughout all this crap, I made one bad move." Kylie paused, taking a deep breath, and Erica could tell what she was going to say was upsetting.

"It's okay. Take your time."

"I found a picture online of a naked guy. I'd been complaining to a friend about everything that was happening and she dared me to hang a naked guy picture in the locker room—so I did. It wasn't any worse than what the men did, but I knew how these guys were, and I knew it would piss them off to see a naked guy in there, so I hung it up. But no one said anything. And I just thought maybe they hadn't noticed.

"But when it was time to leave for the day and I went to my locker, I had a lovely surprise. They'd taken some of their nudie pics and used them like paper dolls, taping them around the picture I'd hung. One picture was made to look like the woman was licking the naked man's rear—they drew a tongue on her—and another woman they had up around his neck. These guys just couldn't let anything go. And that was when I knew I'd made a mistake. So instead of making it worse, I took the pictures down and threw them away.

"And *that* was when I went to the boss. He made a good show of it, acting all concerned and angry, taking notes and stuff. And I knew he couldn't resolve it right away—or at least that's what he said. He said it was a personnel issue and he'd have to talk to HR—and then, at some point, I figured it would get better, you know, when he could actually talk to the guys. But days went by and then weeks, and literally nothing changed. That was when I figured he hadn't done anything."

"Was your boss ever around when any of these things happened?"

There was Brock interrupting again.

"No. He usually just sat in his office doing paperwork. I'm convinced he just didn't care.

"So that's when it got really bad. The jokes got worse and, instead of talking about me like 'this woman,' they just started talking about me like I wasn't there. And they'd say threatening things, like, 'If I was Kylie's boyfriend, I'd fuck her good.' And their jokes got nastier. But the final straw for me was the day I found what I'm pretty sure was semen in my locker."

"What? Please tell me—"

"Did you record it?" Brock interjected. "That should be cause for immediate dismissal."

"I was horrified. Disgusted. Disbelieving that someone would stoop to that level. And I was kind of scared. I went straight to my supervisor then and I decided if he wasn't there or wouldn't do anything, I was either going to go straight to HR or someone else. It was time to punish these guys.

"Well, my supervisor wasn't in his office. I had to search the building and finally found him in the break room talking to another supervisor. I told him he needed to come see something immediately. He blew me off but finally, after much urging, came with me.

"And I think my jaw actually hit the floor—because, by the time we got to my locker, it was gone. My supervisor told me he was tired of me trying to get the guys in trouble, that I was making it up, stirring up shit—and, yes, he used the word *shit*. See? That's the thing...I knew the guys down there were crude, cussing and stuff. I learned that day one. And I didn't want to disrupt anything, but it was oppressive in shipping. It really was."

Erica was content just letting her vent so that she could wind her way through her emotions and the events, but Brock once more intervened. "What happened next?"

And Erica felt even angrier at herself that she was even emotional—that what he was doing had such an effect on her in the first place. It made it harder for her to concentrate on Kylie's words.

"He sent me home for the day. It was time to leave anyway. But he told me to get some rest and think about what I'd done...what I'd accused the men down there of. I was kind of confused at first. Very upset...so upset that I called in sick the next day. I really questioned my sanity but, by the day after, I was convinced my supervisor had to be in on it—or, at the very least, he was aware of it, even though he pointed the finger at me. He was, by far, the worst boss I've ever had. So I decided to go to HR during my lunch break or after work. And, believe me, I *wanted* to go there first thing, but their office didn't open till nine, and I had to report to work by seven. But I figured I could tolerate half a day with those primates before that. I'd just bide my time.

"When I showed up to shipping, though, my boss didn't even let me get to the locker room. He intercepted me at his office and invited me in. Behind closed doors, he told me that he understood I'd been under a lot of stress and that he'd talked with HR and the administrative team, and they'd decided to move me back to QA. 'It's for the best, Kylie,' he said. I signed the papers, cleaned out my locker, and reported for duty in QA, kind of shell shocked. Numb even. And I just pulled up my bootstraps and got to work, but that night at home, I was like, 'I don't *want* to work in QA.' But I stuck it out for a while anyway, while trying to think what to do. I asked my old boss—my *ex*—about it, and he said they told him he had to take me back, and he was all right with that, because I was a good worker. And then when I got my next check, I saw that they had *demoted* me. They changed my pay back to my old QA pay. It might not seem like much, but it was an entire dollar an hour difference. And people were talking about me, too. HR wasn't any help, either. Every time I went to talk to them, they shoved some form in my face. They never actually *listened*."

"So what do you want, Kylie?" Brock asked. "What are you wanting us to sue them for?"

"For justice. This isn't right."

"Let me rephrase, because, either way, if the court decides in your favor, there will be some sort of punishment. You're still working for Pioneer, correct?"

"Yes."

"So do you want monetary damages—for pain and suffering and lost wages—or do you want your old job back? Or all of the above?"

Kylie was silent for a few moments before she said, "I don't know. I hadn't thought about it."

"You don't have to decide right away. We can start putting your case together now and—"

This time Erica interjected. "How much could we get for her? I mean...so she doesn't have to continue working for them." She turned to Kylie. "Unless, of course, you do."

"I don't know. Part of me wants to, because they've been the only real employer I've ever worked for. Before that, in high school, I worked for Burger King and a couple of convenience stores. Pioneer actually offered me benefits and better money, so I'm kind of afraid to leave."

Brock began to talk, but Erica was competing with him now and beat him to the punch. "If you had some compensation from them, though, money to live on, you could find other employment during that time."

Kylie asked, "Do you think I should start looking for other work now?"

"That's entirely up to you, but it's something to consider."

Brock said, "It would probably look better for your case. I don't think, based upon your testimony, it will be hard to prove that you've been subjected to a hostile work environment—particularly if you have documentation or witnesses to back you up."

She shook her head. "I don't really have any witnesses—and I'm pretty sure all those guys would say I was making it all up. They got what they wanted—they got me out of there." She took a phone out of her purse and began swiping. "I have pictures of all that stuff, though."

"What about the semen?"

"No." Kylie frowned as she turned the phone for both Erica and Brock to see the locker room full of nude pictures. The photo on the phone was taken so far back that, even though she could tell it was *probably* a nude woman, she couldn't be sure. "I was so upset, I didn't even think about it." She turned the phone, swiped again, and then there was a picture close up. Yes, there was no mistaking this one. Only it wasn't just a nude woman. It was *two* nude women, one grinding her crotch into the other woman's face.

Erica started to ask a question when Brock said, "Do you have these saved elsewhere? We're going to need copies of them all."

"I was hoping you could put them on your computer."

"We'll have my secretary do that when we're done. And you said you've documented everything?"

"Yes." Kylie held up her notebook.

"We probably have copies of all that, but I'll have my secretary copy your notes as well, just to be sure." Kylie nodded before Brock then turned to Erica. "So what do you think, counselor?"

Oh, *now* he was going to let her talk—when she had no idea. *This* was the part where she could use his help—and he should know that, based on the other clients they'd spoken with earlier that day. What an asshole.

But maybe she knew. "I think it's going to start with a summons and complaint."

"Close. One thing first, though." Ah, so it had been a trick question. He wasn't just an asshole—he was a *fucking* asshole. Was he intentionally trying to make her look bad? But he continued, looking at Kylie, as if he didn't even know what he'd done. "Have you filed a complaint with the EEOC?"

"The *what?* What's that?"

"The Equal Employment Opportunity Commission. You should file with them first. Doing so will cost you nothing but they oftentimes will sue on your behalf."

"Do I *have* to do that?"

Brock's face looked grim. "Well, you don't *have* to, but a judge could dismiss the case outright if you haven't already exhausted that option. The EEOC pulls a lot of weight—and that's their specialty. That's all they do. They make sure your workplace rights aren't being violated...and I can assure you they have been."

"So what should I do?"

"I'll have Harriet help you with all of that. We'll go ahead and make copies of what you have, just so you know it's safe, but you've got to let the EEOC take a stab at it first." Brock leaned forward, creating an *I-care-about-you* feeling with his posture. "They are the experts."

Kylie's face dropped. "So then should I keep working there?"

"That's a personal decision. Only *you* know what you can handle. If you feel safe where you are right now, I think you'll be all right. But I want to assure you that the EEOC really does have your best interests at heart—and they're the experts."

Their young almost ex-client sighed. "So what do I owe you for today?"

"Nothing. We'll return your retainer and can plan to collect it *if* the EEOC drops the ball on this one. But they take charges of a hostile work environment very seriously. You'll be in good hands. I promise." Brock stood then, signaling that they were done.

Erica, still smoldering from the emotional gauntlet she felt like she'd been running through, also felt a little warmth. She never in a million years would have expected to see such a generous gesture from Brock. They'd spent close to half an hour of billable time and could have kept part of Kylie's retainer, especially considering the copies Harriet would be making and the time she'd be spending giving all the EEOC info to Kylie. Her emotions were all up in the air, and she knew it was all because of Brock. Had it been Bret next to her, it probably wouldn't have bothered her at all.

Why was that exactly?

She knew why...it was because of a fire burning in her belly for this man. That hadn't been part of the bargain, and she wasn't quite sure how to handle that....

CHAPTER THIRTEEN

ERICA STOOD IN Brock's office fuming. In fact, she was surprised smoke wasn't streaming out of her ears by the time he got back. She couldn't let the fact that, at the end, he'd proven himself to be a bit of a softie interfere with what she had to say.

He walked in the door, closing it but his eyes were boring straight into Erica. What was that look? What was he thinking?

It didn't matter, because she had to get this shit off her chest. NOW. It didn't matter that he looked fucking hotter than he had in a long while.

"Dammit, Brock. Are you ever going to let me handle my cases myself or are you going to constantly interfere like that?" She could feel her blood pumping, could tell her pupils were dilated, so there was no question that she was pissed off.

His voice was calm and steady when he answered. "*You* weren't going to advise her about filing with the EEOC—and that's probably something we should have asked *first*, long before she got into telling her tale. Hell, the para who staffed it already should have sent her on her way. That case should have been screened out before it got to us."

"Okay, fine," she said, her blood pressure rising. She was digging her nails into her palm just to keep her voice cool. "But earlier in the conversation, why the hell did you keep interrupting?"

Instead of answering her question, he smirked and said, "You're awfully cute when you're angry."

"See? That. *That's* what I'm talking about. You're not taking me seriously." She had to fight herself to stop her voice from rising. "You think I'm incompetent. You probably even think I *deserve* to be stuck doing research."

Why was he moving so close to her?

His voice was low then, barely audible, but her senses were heightened so much that she could have heard a pin drop on the rich carpeting underneath her heels. "That's where you're wrong, Erica." Her heart started beating faster, but surely that was because she was so angry, right? As he took another two steps toward her, every muscle in her body grew taut, as if she was a wind-up toy—and that spring was about to break from the pressure. "I think you're as sharp as they come—and I think you'll make a hell of a litigator." He stopped just inches away from her, so close she was sure she could feel his body heat. "But you need a little guidance. That's why I'm here."

She could hear the fury in her voice, but it couldn't be helped. "You were stepping on my toes the entire time. You didn't even let me *try*." While she continued to talk, Brock's face was getting closer, inching in toward hers. She felt the blood swirling in her veins, her toes curling in her pumps as her body begged for him to do it. In spite of the logical side of her brain wanting to argue, her body wanted his touch, needed to feel him inside her, and that intuitive side of herself sensed that something was about to happen. "I can't—"

Then he did it. His lips collided with hers.

Holy hell.

She'd told him hands off since his first stolen kiss—and she'd meant it—but her body couldn't resist this time, almost melting into him.

Her nostrils were assaulted with the scent of sandalwood while she tasted his tongue as it flicked against hers. Her hands were pressed against his chest as if to push him away, but those naughty betrayers instead crept around his neck and her fingers wound through his hair. The entirety of his solid body pressed against her, and she knew now that she was helpless to resist.

As his lips left her mouth, he growled. "I *can* and I *will*."

She felt breathless. And his sudden bossiness sent a charge down her spine. Her pussy responded, making her panties wet.

But he didn't need to know he had that effect on her. She could still resist.

If that was the case, then why weren't her fingers unwinding from his hair?

And then *oh*…his eyes. She could hardly see the blue of his irises, his pupils were so dark. They weren't shadowed with anger as hers had been; instead, they were full of need, and why that made her stomach clench in anticipation, she didn't dare guess.

Her voice wasn't nearly as strong as she needed it to be if the plan was to fight her urges. "No, you *can't.*" But her eyes had drifted to his lips as her body begged her to give in to her deepest, darkest desires.

"Stop fighting me, Erica. There's no sense in it when I know you want me."

She didn't sound as confident as she'd hoped when she protested. "That's what you think."

Suddenly, his lips were brushing against the delicate flesh of her neck, causing her body to break out in goosebumps. "Your body gives you away." She felt his hot breath as his lips brushed against her skin until he nibbled at her earlobe. "Giving in to your desire doesn't make you weak." He'd found her vulnerable spot. Kisses on her neck were likely her sexual Achilles Heel, and his attention there caused her entire body to heat up, making her insides feel like jelly. She wanted nothing more than to feel him inside her now.

Teetering on the edge of temptation, she knew she was ready to walk down that path of no return—but as his lips left her skin and he raised his head, she decided that if one more arrogant phrase tumbled out of his mouth, she was going to push him away and march out the door, no matter how aroused she felt.

Instead, he pressed his forehead into hers and said, "Just say yes, Erica. It's that easy."

She swallowed, trying to think what this would mean for their relationship if she gave in, but her brain was too fuzzy from desire. It was difficult to concentrate on anything other than his eyes and his hands at her waist. The kicker, though, was when he leaned in closer, because then she was painfully aware of his hardened member pressing into her belly.

That was for *her.* There was no denying it.

She sucked her lower lip into her mouth, trying to stop herself from saying that little three-letter-word, but as his eyes seared into hers and her pussy clenched against itself, pleading with her to give up the fight, she gave a slight nod of her head.

But her hands were already in motion.

His mouth consumed her as her fingers fumbled with the buttons on his shirt. Why she wanted to run her fingers along his chest, she didn't know, but she wasn't going to stop now. His hands slid down and cupped her ass before he lifted her under her thighs. Wrapping her legs around his body felt as natural as breathing, and it was then that she first felt his cock pressed against her lady parts. There was no stopping the spontaneous moan that uttered from her mouth.

"That's it."

His words felt dangerously close to his usual cocky talk, but it was easier to ignore it when she could feel herself already nearing the brink. One black heel fell to the floor and the front of her skirt bunched up at her hips while the rest flowed down her backside, something that would have been impossible had she worn her usual pencil skirt. It was almost like she'd known...

His unbuttoned shirt gave her easy access to his skin underneath. Just as she'd suspected, his muscles were firm and hard, reminding her of his cock relentlessly grinding into her, mimicking the feeling of what couldn't begin soon enough. There was no way her fingers could continue stroking the skin of his abdomen when she needed to feel him in her.

She squeezed her hands into the tight space between their bodies until her fingers were digging at the button on his slacks. He stopped kissing her then to say, "I take it this is a definite yes."

"God, would you just shut up for one fucking minute, Brock?"

"And *cursing* now. Do I have this effect on you?"

"I *said*—" His lips descended upon hers as she felt a fresh surge of anger charge through her body once more.

But her hands betrayed her again. Instead of pushing him away, they finished with the zipper on his slacks and found their way inside until they were stroking his steely length. It was then that she realized he was as close to being out of control as he'd ever get—and then she thought maybe she had as much power in this situation as he did. Her only sign was that his kiss slowed and softened a bit, as if his attention was being drawn from his tongue to what she was doing below.

She slid her right hand inside his underwear, wrapping it

around his cock. His lips slackened as he let out a breath. Yes, she was finally making him feel as wild as she did. "See what you do to me, Erica?" She paused then, opening her eyes, because his voice sounded more sincere than she'd ever heard. Was this the real Brock, the man underneath all the brash arrogance on display? He opened his eyes then and said, "I've wanted you since we kissed at dad's party."

She was afraid of saying anything then, because she was sure he was nothing but a player. But it didn't matter. She wanted him now—her body *needed* him now—and she was willing to accept whatever consequences came after. But she didn't want to seem vulnerable or delicate. This was part of the business deal, nothing more.

"So what the hell are you waiting for?"

His eyes assessed hers once more as he lowered her to the ground. She felt her heart drop, because this was the ultimate rejection—getting her steamed up past the point of no return, only to toss her aside.

Or so she'd thought. Instead, he said, "Take off your panties."

She didn't think twice about obeying this subtle order, and she slid the lacy black things down her thighs, painfully aware of how wet they'd become. As she stood, kicking away her other shoe, she saw Brock, wallet in hands, fishing out a square packet before tossing it to the floor and tearing the packet open. Erica felt her mouth flood with saliva as she watched him roll the condom over his cock. By now, his pants were loose and all but sliding down his legs. As he bunched one side of her skirt in his fist, she expected him to lift her up again so he could pummel her at last, but he instead slid his other hand between her legs, running a finger up her slit.

There was no denying her response.

"Say you want me, Erica."

A trace of the anger she'd felt earlier reared its ugly head. "Why do you need me to say it? Can't you tell?"

His jaw clenched. God, that was sexier than he knew, because it made him look a little intimidating. Maybe he was just like her—all these pent-up emotions she couldn't deny, couldn't fight. There was no winning.

"It's not the same." He swirled his finger against her clit, causing a charge to rush through her body.

"Stop playing, Brock." She could hear the desperation in her voice as need coursed through her veins.

He punctuated his words with another swirl, and her pussy clenched in response. "Say it."

She felt like she was going to die, and it was true—she wanted Brock now more than she'd ever wanted another thing in her whole damn life, and if he was going to refuse just because she wouldn't say it…well, then it was time for her to stop being stubborn, to stop fighting him over everything.

Just this one tiny thing…the one thing he wanted.

But she wasn't going to be sweet about it. "I want you to fuck me, Brock, and I want you to do it now."

The fierceness of her voice surprised her, but his response did not. His mouth consumed hers as he lifted her up against the wall. She spread her legs, ready to take him inside her, eager to feel him fill her. As he slid his cock inside her walls with primitive fierceness, she heard a moan escape her mouth.

Why had she fought him so hard?

She was on the brink already, and each stroke brought her closer. Something in the wall behind her was poking her in the back, distracting her, keeping her from that moment where she could let go, but she could tell now that Brock too was painfully near the edge. She adjusted her back, causing her core to grind against him and that change of angle was all it took. Her mind slid into madness as the earth shattered around her like bits of tinkling glass, and she buried her lips against his neck, hoping to muffle her cries of deliriousness, lest anyone in the building find out.

"God, Erica." Those were his last words as he let go, his thrusts slowing as he drowned in pleasure.

For a few moments, all she could hear was their heavy breathing as they wound down.

And the earth had not stopped moving while they'd been otherwise engaged. The intercom on the table buzzed, reminding them they had much work to do. "Mr. Ford, your next appointment is here. Shall I bring them back?"

He raised his voice. "We need another few minutes to finish up in here." As the secretary responded through the intercom once more, Brock stroked Erica's cheek with his thumb. His eyes seemed softer for the moment, but in another five seconds, he was completely back to business—and back to his usual arrogant self. "Feel better now?"

As his brain cleared, he realized that he saw Erica in a whole new light. Yes, she was smart, beautiful, sassy—but they were also compatible. He'd never had sex like that before. Awesome sex? Yes. Even shitty sex, so long as it culminated in climax, was good enough—but soul connecting love making was something else entirely.

He could honestly say he'd never before felt this way after copulation.

What the hell was going on inside his head?

Was it because she'd said she really wanted him? Yes, it was under duress…but he believed it just the same. Erica was the kind of woman who would have refused had it not been true, on the verge of orgasm or not. She was too stubborn to give in with a lame lie.

No way could he let her know what the fuck he was feeling now. Even he didn't quite understand it—and, besides, this shit wasn't supposed to happen. It wasn't part of the deal. She was supposed to help him continue his bachelorhood, not make him want to be hitched to a girlfriend.

But that was okay. As soon as they could "call off" the engagement, he could settle back into his old life.

His slacks were zipped up and he ran his fingers through his hair while Erica tucked, smoothed, and pulled her clothing back into shape. As he came to his senses, he wondered to himself what the hell appointment he had waiting for him. He went to the desk and pressed on the intercom button on his phone. When Harriet answered, he asked, "What appointment do we have waiting? I thought we were done for the day."

"Mrs. Fierro is here, remember? She had some questions about the deposition tomorrow and you were going to meet with her this afternoon."

He vaguely remembered telling his client to come in "sometime after work"—*her* job in which her hours varied. "Okay. We need just a couple more minutes. I'll let you know." He hung up and then said to Erica, "You might as well stay for this appointment, too. I can go over the things I usually tell clients when they're put under oath—it's something you need to know."

That was good. Calm, collected—like nothing had happened a few minutes ago.

Like they hadn't both just had the best fucking sex of their lives.

"No, thank you. I have to go."

"What?" He walked over to the desk and wiggled the mouse to wake his computer back up.

"I said I have to go."

She was fiddling with her shoe, and it seemed as though she was doing it just as a refusal to make eye contact with him. "We have work to do here, Erica."

Then she stood up, her earthy eyes full of venom. "No, *you* have work to do. I don't know anything about your client. The people we interviewed today? Any discussions we might need to have about their cases will wait till morning." She marched over to his desk and picked up the files and legal pad she'd been taking notes on before shoving a pen in the crook of her ear.

There was that feisty streak that, by God, he was not willing to tamp out. It was becoming one of the things he loved the most about her, especially because her defiance was sexy as hell. Was it *because* something inside him wanted to break through that, capture her heart despite her stubbornness? He didn't know.

Fortunately, he'd had years and years of practice at remaining calm in courtroom after courtroom amidst flying emotions. This was nothing. His voice was as smooth as silk when he said, "What makes you think I won't fire you for leaving without permission?"

Her hand on the doorknob, she turned. Her head was tilted, her lips curled in a smirk when she answered. "Go ahead. You do that, I'll call off the engagement. Simple." And, without waiting for a reply, she marched through the door and shut it—firmly but without slamming it. He sensed restraint—and some undercurrent he couldn't quite pick up on, particularly because it was hard to focus. His body was still swimming with endorphins and some stupid lovey-dovey reaction. He had to find his balls so he could focus on his client.

But, first, he had to will down the semi-erection that had perked up when Erica had shown more fire. This woman was gonna kill him. His dick thought it was fifteen years old again.

Drink of water. One walk around the office. Thoughts of sitting in a boring deposition with a bland court reporter and a know-it-all attorney.

He was set.

"Harriet, please send in Mrs. Fierro now."

Business first. Contemplation later.

Brock was back in the office at seven, still having worked in two miles and a light breakfast afterward. He was on his third cup of coffee an hour later when Erica strolled into the room. Yes, she'd rapped on his door but hadn't waited for him to invite her in.

He knew it was her, but she was going to have to wait before he looked up from his work. He wanted her now, more than ever, but there was no way he was going to let her know that. He'd thought about her all night—the way her skin had tasted under his tongue, the way her pussy had gripped his cock like she'd been waiting all her life for him, the way she'd dug her fingernails into the flesh of his neck like she was claiming him as hers.

Push those goddamn thoughts out.

Cool and calm. He didn't even raise his eyes off the papers he was perusing. "Yes?"

Her voice was as cold as an ice cube. "I need to ask you some questions about one of the cases from yesterday."

He looked up then and saw that her face was as frozen as her words. She was still as beautiful as ever, but her hair was pulled back tightly, her makeup stark and severe. Her gray dress was somber, communicating as much as her voice. But she was either pretending to ignore what had happened between them yesterday or she was angry about it. Either way, there were emotions there she was trying to pretend weren't there—and that was probably a good thing. It likely meant that it had seemed like more to her, too.

So no way in hell was he going to go easy on her. No way.

He straightened his back as though he'd been hunched over this particular case file for days and said, "Hmm. You need my help already, huh?"

Her eyes began to glower again, a look he loved entirely too much. "If you'd rather, I can make a misstep and let the firm pay for it."

He smiled, suppressing a laugh. "Relax. Sit down and let's take a look at it." Acting as though she wasn't sure she wanted to, she reluctantly sat in a chair on the other side of the desk. "Have you had coffee yet?"

She nodded but wasn't interested in small talk. "So the Frahley case, the one where she was working overtime but not clocking in and out?"

Brock didn't forget cases, but now was not the time to say so. "Yes, I recall."

"You know how she said it started out with her deciding to clock out before counting the drawer or when she'd already gone over the time she should have?" Brock nodded. "So I called her yesterday afternoon and asked her when her employer started *requiring* her to do it. She said it was voluntary for about a year and it's been the last six months that they've been making her—because when she stayed clocked in, it was her actual time, which took quite a bit longer than when she gave them time for free."

"So what's your question?"

"I clarified because I thought maybe we could only sue from the time the employer knew...but the law—"

"You're right. It doesn't matter. They're liable either way—but it's even worse with them being fully aware and demanding it."

"You're doing it again, Brock."

He was going to play innocent. She didn't realize that, while they were working, every minute was money—so he tended to rush through things that didn't matter. Technically, yes, Erica could bill for the case she was working on, but her rate wasn't as high as his. "What?"

"Interrupting. It's awfully rude."

No apologizing. No giving away how he really felt about her. "I knew what you were going to say, Erica. In this business, time is money." Her brows furrowed, the inside corners of her eyes squinting. "Am I wrong? Was there something else you needed to get off your chest?"

She was holding her tongue, much like he'd spent his entire life doing with his family, and he could see her grappling with her emotions and thoughts. Finally, she said, "No." Her eyes were searching his and he couldn't help but wonder what the hell she was thinking—and what the fuck was wrong with him. Jesus. It wasn't like he'd never had sex before—great sex, amazing sex, mind-blowing rip-the-sheets-off-the-bed sex. What the hell was going on with him? Why couldn't he stop thinking about her that way?

He needed to focus on work and get her out of his head, but she interrupted his thoughts. "I just want to know why you're being such an asshole."

Brock couldn't help the chuckle that tumbled out of his mouth. "*Asshole?* What did I do to deserve that moniker? You don't appreciate honesty?"

"I don't mind honesty—but you can do that without being a jerk."

It wasn't going to be good if he gave away how amused he was, so he tried to make sure his face looked more serious. "If it makes you feel better, I can try."

He could tell she almost smiled. "That's all I ask." After a cleansing breath, she asked, "So what are *you* working on?"

"I've got a trial tomorrow that I'm preparing for."

"Why don't you tell me about it? It's good for me to learn strategy."

"I don't know how much strategy you'll get from me. This is pretty cut and dry...but come on over." No, he didn't really need for her to look at his computer screen or the file to get an idea of what he was referring to, but he wasn't going to miss the chance. She wore some spicy perfume—he had no idea what the notes were, because fragrances weren't his thing, but it reminded him of cinnamon or cloves with a touch of pepper and maybe even a pinch of sugar. Most women he'd dated wore floral scents—of course, leave it to Erica to be a little different. "My client owns several restaurants in Arapahoe County. He's been accused of murdering his wife."

"And you're defending him?"

"Yes. All I have to do is plant doubt in the jury's mind, because the burden of proof is on the state. Most of what they have is circumstantial. She fell over one hundred feet off a cliff in Rocky Mountain National Park to her death."

"Was he with her?"

"He said he lost track of her—that they'd been hiking and he'd paused to take some pictures with his phone. He heard her screaming and ran over to see her falling to her death."

"Oh, that poor man."

Brock couldn't help the smirk spreading across his face. "Not so fast. His first wife apparently died suspiciously, drowning in a pool at a resort in Las Vegas while my client slept through the night."

"Maybe he's just unlucky."

"Can I have you on my jury?"

"Seriously, though. The man's lost two wives. That must hurt."

"Well...he had her covered with five million dollars in life insurance."

"Wow. That seems excessive."

"The police thought so, too. It didn't help that he had a map with markings on it, markings that end about the place where his wife fell to her untimely death. And her friends and family say the last thing she ever would have wanted to do was hike."

"Ouch. So you think—?"

"I think the man needs an attorney. And that's why I'm here." He closed the file folder. His arguments weren't going to get any stronger. He was going to push the fact that all the cops had was circumstantial evidence—and conflicting statements from his client.

"Did he have pictures on his phone? You know...to corroborate his statement that he was off shooting pictures while she was slipping on a ledge or whatever?"

"Actually, he *does*. But investigators think those were taken afterward."

"Can they prove it?"

"I don't know. I guess I'll find out later this week." He smiled at her. "But I think I need to try to lean toward a female jury. He's the crushed widower who's had the misfortune of losing not one but two wives in his lifetime—and here we are making a mockery of it." His eyes lit up. "I wonder how big an insurance policy he had on himself." Snapping his fingers, he said, "That's it. Thank you, Erica."

He wanted to kiss her right then and there. She was gorgeous, and just engaging in discussion about the case had helped him come up with what could be a perfect defense—provided his dumb ass client had either no life insurance or a small one for a couple hundred thousand.

"I guess I'll get out of your hair."

Erica began to stand when Brandon walked in the door. "Ah, just the people I wanted to see. Lisa wondered if both of you would like to come to our place for dinner tonight. She said she loves Erica and really wants to get to know her better. Oh, and if you say no, I'll have hell to pay." He smiled and then said, "But no pressure."

Brock looked at Erica while saying, "It works for me, but I don't know what Erica's got on tap. I need to be home relatively early since I have the Cool trial tomorrow."

"Already?"

"Yeah."

"Good luck, bro. I know you'll kick ass."

Brock tried not to let his jaw hit the floor, because this was one of the first genuine compliments Brandon had given him as an adult. It was...touching, to say the least. "Thanks, Bran."

Erica said, "Yeah. I think that works for me. Besides, I need to give Saffy a kiss. I miss that little sweetie."

"Lisa will be thrilled to hear it. See you guys around—I dunno—seven tonight?"

Both agreed before Brandon slipped away. "Thanks, Erica. I appreciate it."

She turned to him, jabbing her pointy finger into his chest—and why did his cock consider perking up at that? With a hiss, she said, "But *No. More. Sex.*" A smile spread his cheeks wider than it should have. "Keep your dick in your pants."

He put his hands up and said, "Whatever you say."

"Pick me up around six-thirty?"

"Try six. We've got rush hour traffic to contend with, and they live in Highlands Ranch."

"I'd say it's a date, but I don't need you getting any more bright ideas."

"Yes, ma'am." And he wondered, as he watched her fine ass sashay out of his office, just exactly how he could go about making her his—or if that was even a possibility.

CHAPTER FOURTEEN

ERICA WAS MOST definitely along for the ride, but she didn't know how much longer she could keep up with this charade. This afternoon had finally settled back into something she might call "normal" when it came to the relationship between her and Brock, but it had been strange and weird at first. Finally just ignoring their indiscretion, she was able to concentrate on what mattered most—her career.

But that indiscretion—holy hell, it had been too damn good. And, in spite of the fact that it had been hurried, upright, and all but fully clothed, she could admit to herself that it was some of the best sex she'd ever had. She'd been analyzing it over the past twenty-four hours and come to the conclusion that Brock was an amazing lover. He'd known which of her buttons to press and he'd read her like a book.

He was a genius when it came to her body—but she'd never admit it to him in a million years. In fact, it made her despise him all the more.

Traffic was bumper to bumper and slow but not at a standstill as they made their way down C-470 for the last little stretch. Five minutes later, though, Brock was winding down a quiet road. On all sides, even though they were shrouded by darkness, the street lamps were able to illuminate ostentatious homes—not quite mansions, but Erica knew just by looking that these places were easily worth half a million or even double that, way out of her present price range. But why would that be surprising? One of the reasons she'd settled on becoming an attorney (as opposed to, say, a private investigator or a college professor) was that, once they'd paid their dues, they made bank. This wealthy neighborhood Brock's brother had chosen for his home gave her hope for the future.

Brock pulled in front of a beautiful house adorned with either multicolored bricks or flat stones—she couldn't tell which in the low light—but it was breathtaking. Two stories and a two-car garage were adorned by lovely though bare shade trees in the front and short well-manicured bushes inside a modest flower bed nestled up against the house. From the front, the place looked like what Erica would consider normal, but from the side, she saw that the house went far back, and she couldn't even calculate how many rooms that might possibly mean, but her guess was that it was between three and four thousand square feet. She knew her apartment wasn't even one thousand. Hell, she'd be lucky if it was eight hundred.

Brock continued to play the gentleman, holding the door open for her and taking her hand to assist her getting out of the car. She'd changed into jeans and a sweater, hoping her supposed in-laws wouldn't mind if she enjoyed her downtime. And even though he was wearing his standard black leather jacket, she could see that Brock was also wearing jeans, paired with a long-sleeved cotton shirt that didn't quite cling but certainly emphasized his musculature.

Damn him for being so yummy.

Brandon answered the door. "Perfect timing, guys. We're just about ready." After closing the door behind them, he said, "I'll take your coats." While Brock and Erica stood in the foyer, Brandon walked inside a small doorway to the left. "Either of you need to use the restroom?"

Erica followed Brock as he walked toward where Brandon had turned. He was hanging their coats inside a closet, but she saw that there was also a room beyond him as well as a bathroom behind. Both of them declined using the facilities and, when Brandon finished with their coats, he clapped his hands together. "We're so thrilled you decided to join us."

Now, Erica was no psychologist...and, while she thought part of what Brandon had to say was genuine, she also got the feeling that his being *thrilled* was a bit of an exaggeration. Smooth Brock answered, "It's our pleasure. Thanks for the invitation."

Brandon smiled, all charm. That was one thing the Ford brothers had in common—charisma by the bucket load. "Well, I think Lisa's got a bit of an ulterior motive." Lowering his voice as they walked into the spacious dining room, he said, "She wants to get to know you better, Erica, since you're going to be her ally here very soon."

Ally? What—like it was girls against boys? But no way was she going to ask, because she wasn't really going to be part of the family soon—she merely had to keep playing the charade a little longer.

Lisa walked in from the left, Saffy in her arms. Her dark brown hair was pulled up into a ponytail, making her look a little younger than normal. Smells of broiled veggies, delicate meat in sauces, and gourmet gravies wafted through the doorway, making Erica's mouth water, reminding her that she'd been so busy, she'd forgotten to eat lunch. "So glad you guys came," she said, walking first to Brock, who took baby Saffy in his arms after kissing Lisa on the cheek, and then over to Erica. She hugged her and then kissed her cheek. "You look gorgeous as always."

"Thanks, Lisa. You look great, too. Do you need any help in the kitchen?"

The other woman laughed. "No. My cook left just a few minutes ago and I just had to transfer it all to serving dishes. I guess you could help me bring it all out to the table."

Erica agreed, and they made a few trips back and forth. The kitchen was huge, white, and spotless, with a morning room toward the back with a huge window facing the cozy back yard. What Erica loved most about their home was the high ceilings that made the rooms feel even more spacious. And the kitchen was perfect.

But it couldn't compare to the dining room. The center of attention was a large dark hardwood table surrounded by eight upholstered chairs, all with intricately carved edges. This place *felt* expensive, especially with the beautiful hutch full of china and liquor bottles, a Persian rug on the floor, and a window covering that probably cost more than she'd made in three months. She could hardly breathe, thanks to the overwhelm, but she looked forward to the meal nonetheless. Spending time with Brock's family over the past month, she'd discovered her palate could easily become spoiled by the fine food they consumed.

By the time they were all seated, Brandon had filled their glasses with wine. They also had glasses for water and two carafes were filled to the brim. Lisa set Saffy on a blanket on the floor, surrounded by toys and a bottle. "I fed her earlier, so please don't think I'm starving her," she said to Erica. "She couldn't wait to eat."

"Smelling all this, I can see why," Erica joked.

They passed platters and bowls around the table, and soon her plate was filled with a slice of prime rib in a savory sauce, a baked potato she'd loaded with butter and sour cream, asparagus spears, and steamed broccoli. She also had a small bowl of salad made of various greens and cherry tomatoes sprinkled with a lemon vinaigrette and, next to it, a small plate with a slice of crusty French bread. If she'd been at home with her parents, she would have been chowing down, but she knew she had to be dainty and take her time with these people who ate in a more refined, patient manner. It wasn't that she was a pig but that she enjoyed food.

Soon, they were all eating and making light conversation—about a snowstorm that was going to blanket the Denver area that weekend, a dispute case Brandon was buried in, and how Saffy was crawling all over the place, probably close to walking soon. But halfway through the meal, Lisa said, "Erica, I would be honored if you'd let me help you plan your wedding." Erica raised her eyebrows but continued chewing the piece of prime rib between her molars. "I helped Bret and Elle, because I didn't get much say in my own wedding." As if they were being recorded, she dropped her voice to a whisper. "My mother domineered my entire ceremony, so I'm kind of experiencing the joy by helping my future sisters-in-law."

Erica had to remind herself that none of this was real. She wasn't going to marry Brock, nor was she going to become part of this family. In the short time she'd spent with her supposed fiancé's family, she had pegged Brandon and Lisa to be the ones most concerned with money, and their home just kind of confirmed that. During the meal she'd learned that the house was three stories instead of two and the garage housed three cars instead of a couple—not that they needed a space that big. They had expensive taste and it showed. Either Brandon made a million or more a year or they were in debt up to their ears—but they could afford it. Easily. They were all about money and appearances, finery and fashion, and even though Lisa seemed nice enough, her adoration of brand names Erica had never even heard of and her worship of gold and dollar bills grated on her nerves. So while the wedding wasn't even a real thing, the idea that Lisa would put her into debt without a blink of her eyelashes for a ceremony Erica would likely loathe made her feel backed into a corner.

It's not real, she had to remind herself.

The longer Lisa talked about multi-tiered wedding cakes, melt-in-your-mouth wedding mints, a white chapel-length train on a wedding gown adorned in lace and pearls, an orchestra, various venues, menus, and the like, the more Erica was beginning to hate the conversation.

She wouldn't have been able to marry into this family. She couldn't be that person.

Brock, who'd been engaged in a side conversation with his brother, happened to glance over and overheard what was going on. "You know, Lisa," he said, and Erica looked to her left, interested in hearing what he had to add, "Erica and I haven't talked about the actual wedding. I realize we should, but we just barely made it official. But if I had to guess," he said, his face full of arrogant charm, sending a bolt of lightning zipping through every tendril of Erica's nerves, "Erica doesn't want a huge, ostentatious, pretentious wedding. Giving it some thought, I know she'd prefer to elope somewhere—like having a small wedding on the Mediterranean on a week-long cruise or maybe a small ceremony on a beach in Hawaii."

Wow. How the hell had Brock nailed it so well? It was like he could see inside her soul, knew the essence of her. He'd discovered that, if and when she ever found the right guy she wanted to attach herself to for life, she wanted something simple and beautiful and romantic to commemorate the moment—not something cheap and flashy or even over-the-top monied and flashy.

Did Brock already understand that about her? Did he already know her that well?

At first, when she looked at him, she was certain he could read all that inside her eyes—and the smirk on his face confirmed it. So she cocked an eyebrow as if to tell him, *Don't think you've got my number, mister.* But she needed to let him know that, yes, he was right—and maybe then Lisa would stop rambling on and on about all the shit she thought Erica would need for an overpriced ceremony. "Yeah, I'd love that actually."

Brock smiled then and brushed her cheek with the back of his knuckles. He was full of genuine sweetness at that moment—enough that Erica knew Brandon and Lisa would fall for the entire act. Finally, he turned his head to his sister-in-law and said, "Sorry. I don't think we want the big wedding, Lisa."

"Brock, Erica…" Lisa said, waiting until they both looked at her, "that's really not fair to your family, you know? They're going to want to participate."

"We didn't say anything about no participation, Lisa, but we don't need everybody whose anybody to participate in our wedding. It's not like they care anyway."

Brock went one step further than Erica, though, when he said, "I don't care. This isn't about them."

Brandon, who'd been quiet up until this point, stepped in. "Not cool, Brock. I don't know why you gotta pull out one of your old tricks."

"What old tricks?"

"Selfishness. Immaturity."

This is about my bride and what *she* wants. If she wants a small wedding, she gets it."

"Blaming it on the bride?"

Brock rolled his eyes and polished off the wine in his glass. "You should just be happy I'm getting married."

Brandon finally laughed. "True."

The rest of the meal felt strained, but at least Lisa changed the subject to home décor. It was evident she knew a lot about the subject, considering their beautifully decorated home.

A couple of hours later, Erica and Brock were finally heading out. Coats on, they left the house, porch light shining their way toward his car parked on the street. Before Brock opened Erica's door for her, he said, "I don't think my brother's buying you and me. A couple of things he asked me when he and I were alone in his study made me realize he's still on the fence about it."

"Even with all the wedding discussion?"

"Yeah."

"What else can we do?"

"To begin with, I think we need to engage in a little more

PDA. That would add credibility to our case."

"Hmm."

"Like right now." Brock was up close, gazing in her eyes with the house behind him. "I'll bet my brother is watching us right now. Can you see?"

Over his shoulder, Erica could see the house clearly, and—just as Brock suspected—Brandon was looking through the thin window beside the door. "Yeah, he is."

"Then we need to kiss to make this believable."

She searched his eyes. Was he full of shit? Did Brandon really care? At this point, it didn't matter. Heaven help her—she wanted Brock to kiss her...to kiss her like tomorrow would never come. So she nodded slightly, feeling her lips part a fraction in anticipation. As his face neared hers one centimeter at a time, she moved forward as well until their lips touched, and it was as if she could feel the molecules exploding as they collided with one another. It was pure magic, and her entire body hummed while his tongue tickled and teased. As if her hands belonged to someone else, she felt her fingers winding through his hair, a small groan forming in her throat, reminding her that she wanted this man again. One more time.

Just until the engagement was off.

Oh, this was not good. Not good at all.

The way she kissed him back, he wouldn't have believed for a second she was only pretending. The connection felt too real, too genuine, and that little noise she let out was certainly not for Brandon's benefit. His brother couldn't hear them out there in the cold.

But *shit*. Not that he would ever tell her, but he knew it himself. It wasn't just one sided. Brock, too, was feeling something, a lot more than he should.

What the hell was wrong with him? Hell, no. This shouldn't be happening. A serious relationship was not on the agenda. Hadn't been. His life plan included marriage—but not till his late thirties or early forties, even. He still had plenty of bachelorhood to make his way through, and no matter how enticing Ms. Erica Larson was, he was not going to allow himself to fall for her.

Deep down, though, he knew—it was far too late. He'd already fallen. The question was if he could pick himself back up.

Yes. Yes, he could. Just because he was falling didn't mean he was hopeless. If Erica would stop looking at him like that, it'd be a hell of a lot easier. And he knew just how to get under her skin. As he opened his eyes, he saw that hers had a dreamlike quality to them. Even in the semi-dark of the street lights, he could see that. "Thanks, babe, but you didn't have to give an Academy Award performance. A simple kiss would have sufficed."

He could feel her muscles stiffen under his arms through her coat, could see the slight flare of her nostrils before the air she huffed out turned white in the cold, and she pushed against him slightly. "I was just following your lead, Brock. Apparently, you thought you needed to convince the jury." She turned, pulling on the door handle that wasn't opening because the car was still locked. "But the jury already got bored and left."

He turned and saw that, indeed, Brandon had left the foyer—had even shut off the porch light. Pressing his fob so the door would open, he tried to reach the door handle so he could open it for her, but she wasn't about to let him near it. He waited until she was seated inside the car before walking over to his side.

The seat was cold, but he could fix that in short order. He hadn't noticed the chill before but now that it was coming from both the air and radiating off Erica's body, he couldn't help but feel it down to his bones. But maybe that was what he needed—because, if not, his very life was in danger.

His life as a bachelor, that was.

The ride was stiff and quiet and the longer it went on that way, the more he felt like a real Grade A asshole.

Both of them were contemplating a next move or the future or…well, he didn't know quite what *she* was thinking. He was guessing, but he knew what was wrong with *him*. He kept reminding himself that he only had to make it one more month. Once the paperwork was finalized, this charade could be over and he could go back to his normal self.

There was just one problem…he didn't *want* to.

He asked it again: What the hell was wrong with him?

Whatever it was, it led him to what happened next in the parking lot. Before he could open her door—and before she let herself out in a huff—he touched her arm until she looked up at him. "Hey, Erica. I'm really sorry."

Her voice was full of venom. "Sorry for *what?*"

Time to own it. "For being an ass. I'm not going to explain why I go there sometimes, but I do want to apologize for acting like a jerk. You're helping me out…and I need to let you know I'm grateful for that."

Even in the darkness in the car, he could see her features soften. That was for the best. Right now, some strange part of him was thinking about her as a long-term girlfriend, but the rest of him—the part he'd called an ass—wanted him to cut ties now, to stop acting like a lovesick schoolgirl. He couldn't allow himself the luxury of having a girlfriend or of being attached. He was too young and far too busy to go there right now. There would be plenty of time in the future when he didn't have so damn much to prove.

"I want to walk you to the front doors. I know this is a good neighborhood and I'm not really your fiancé, but I'd feel better doing it, even if you're mad at me."

He could barely hear her voice when she replied, "I'm *not* mad at you."

He got out and then helped her out on her side, only a little surprised when she let him keep his hand on her lower back. He wanted to say something but knew that probably anything out of his mouth at this point would sound like bullshit.

In the quiet walk across the parking lot, he looked up at the sky. The low-hanging clouds were pink, light, and bright, signaling that snow was imminent. When he imagined that Erica would enjoy that, he smiled and then immediately chastised himself. What the hell was he doing? He needed to stop. He was acting like a wide-eyed puppy, and one of them was going to get hurt. It would likely be him if he didn't knock that shit off right now. Erica was likely okay, because she'd gone into this whole matter knowing it was an act. They were engaging in an adult version of the kids' imaginative game of playing house. Except today the homes, clothes, and ages of the participants were real—and so were their hearts.

He was falling in love with Erica Larson and bewildered as to how to stop himself.

Erica herself wasn't making things any better. When they got to the top step leading to the doors of the building, she held her keys but paused from sliding them into the lock. "Do you want to come up for a few minutes?"

Holy fuck. Any other real date and he'd know exactly what that meant. An invitation for a short visit or a cup of coffee translated into sex in his world, and he imagined that was what it meant for Erica. Yes, there were the occasional dates who literally meant talking or drinking coffee, but most times those phrases were euphemisms for getting it on.

And there was no denying that he desperately wanted to get it on with this woman, his pretend fiancée.

There was no way he could say no.

She opened the outer doors and slipped her tiny hand in his. He saw an elevator down the hall, but she pulled him up the stairs—which meant that there would be no elevator foreplay.

When she unlocked the door to her apartment and flipped on the light switch, he quickly glanced around, trying to get a feel for the woman underneath it all. But that was silly. He already knew her. Yes, he could get to know her better, but it wasn't like she'd ever hidden herself. Still, he wanted to discover her secrets.

Except she had other things on her mind. She practically tackled him, wrapping her arms around his neck and forcing him to kiss her with singular passion. These two might not really be the ideal couple, but they were compatible enough in bed, and he couldn't wait to feel her again.

And now, at least, there was no question in his mind as to her feelings. Certainly, she might be hate-fucking him—he knew that—but he suspected there was something else going on there as well, and he figured it was along the lines of what he'd been thinking, too.

But that was imagination, trying to fill in blanks that didn't exist, attempting to assign emotion where none existed. Erica had made no secret of the fact that she despised Brock and everything his family stood for—money, wealth, and even the fact that he himself defended criminals. Maybe, though, she was able to work out her anger and frustration this way, making it a win-win—and when they told the news of a broken engagement to his family, that would be the end of any tryst they might be tempted to partake in.

For now, though, it was okay—because they were playing the roles they'd agreed upon when they'd first decided to go through with this ruse.

God…she tasted so sweet. He'd never suckled a woman's lips quite as supple or delectable as hers. And what he loved about her lips were that they were both soft and pliable yet firm and demanding at the same time. When they ended the second kiss, he'd swear she was already breathless—a hell of a turn on for a guy like Brock—and although he loved the fast pace of their foreplay, he wanted to slow it down…because he knew somehow that this was going to be the last time. He'd never get another chance to touch her sweet flesh. So as their kiss brought them up for air, caused them to pause a bit and put a few hair widths between their lips, he sucked on her bottom one, pulling it into his mouth to his teeth before running his tongue along it. Her eyelids fluttered then, as if she couldn't take any more, but he had so much more to do to her.

He deepened the next kiss then, his tongue pressing firmly against hers, not letting her gasp for air but demanding all her attention, all her focus, and he knew he had it when the fingers in his hair began to pull as if she could no longer control the response of her muscles.

Without thinking clearly, his hand that had been cupping her hipbone pushed her, nearly slamming her into the wall. It was then that he heard her breath as if he'd winded her, but he looked in her eyes and saw that she demanded so much more of him, much like a succubus ready to suck his soul dry. She groaned as he moved his hand up underneath her sweater with rough force, practically begging him to take her. Her pupils were wide, as if she were frightened, but there wasn't a scared bone in her body. She was ready to take him.

Pulling her sweater up to her neck, he yanked her bra down with his other hand. Yes, he should be gentle, but he wanted to send the message that, for the moment, at any rate, she was his. There would be no more thinking about money or his family, cases or the morality of defending someone, winter or summer, engagement or break up. There was only now and the whole of their pleasure, and he was going to take what was his, even if it was only for the night.

So even though the bra clung to her frame, tight and ungiving, her breast still peeked out above it and he pulled her areola into his mouth, its rigid bumpy flesh responding to his tongue. The nipple, firm and erect, seemed to wilt at his touch, and Erica gasped, her fingers again gripping his hair. He let go of her sweater and snuck his thumb up underneath the elastic of her bra to play with the other nipple and it was then that she thrust forward, as if he could not take her breast far enough into his mouth. Another moan, followed by a whispered "Oh, Brock," caused his cock to stand up and take note.

He slid his mouth off her breast, making a trail to her cleavage while he growled, "God, my name on your lips sounds so damn sexy."

Her breathless reply came as she shoved against him. "Shut up."

He kneaded her nipple between thumb and forefinger and replied, "Truth hurts?"

"Just shut up and fuck me, Brock."

"No...not that simple this time. I am going to taste of your sweet nectar just one time, my love."

Erica burst into laughter then, but it sounded desperate, as if she'd been backed into a corner. "Nectar? Is that the best you can come up with?"

He scooped her up into his arms, the light thing that she was, and looked straight into her eyes. "Just tell me if the bedroom's this way."

She moved her head just slightly so that she could see behind her. "Yes. That doorway right there."

He was going to say something else and figured he sounded far more domineering when he kept his mouth shut—and kept her guessing what was coming next. Once inside the room, he practically tossed her on the bed, her chest heaving. He knew her all too well—she was on the verge of demanding he leave, but that wasn't an option. So he leaned over her quickly and captured her mouth with another kiss. Mumbling against her lips, he said, indicating her bra and sweater, "Take these damn things off."

While she was complying, he stood up and pulled first his shirt off, followed by shoes and pants. His cock strained against his underwear, especially when he looked down and saw her lovely, creamy white flesh up against her burgundy bedspread. Pulling his underwear down, he let her gaze upon his erection, pleased at her reaction, and he began to stroke it slowly up and down. "This is for you, princess. But I want to take you to heaven before I pound you with this."

Typically stubborn and disobedient, something he secretly loved, instead of lying back, she sat up and licked the precum off the tip of his cock. Then it was his turn to let out a moan. "Oh, fuck, Erica." But she pulled it into her mouth, just the tip, rubbing the underside with her tongue, making his heart beat faster. "Mmm." He could have let her mouth bring him to climax after sucking him off, but that wasn't what he'd wanted to do. So he moved backwards, sliding his cock out of her mouth, despite the suction she was using to keep him hitting the back of her throat. Then he touched the bottom of her chin with his fingertips. "Come here."

Fluttering her eyelashes, she obeyed, sitting up on her knees, her pink nipples pert and at attention. He'd had one goal when he'd brought her into her bedroom, and he'd thus far failed at it, thanks to her distraction. After another magical kiss, he eased her onto her back and began kissing a trail down the middle of her body. As his tongue created a slick path between her breasts, he brushed one rigid nipple with his fingertips, as if assuring himself that she was still primed and ready. He began kissing her flat tummy on his way down her torso, drawing in little nips of her flesh, meant to tease and prolong the desire, hoping to make for an explosive orgasm later. He could sense that, just underneath the surface, she was on the verge of writhing, which meant he was doing his job well.

Soon, he was between her legs, his face even with the area he intended to give his full attention to. He could see her pussy glistening under the muted light of her room, signaling to him that she was definitely ready for his touch.

But he wanted to test it, so he teased her slit with a light, feathery stroke of his tongue.

Ah, yes, the way she moaned and the tenseness in her thighs told him he could do no wrong here. But enough playing. He wanted to make her scream his name—but, unlike the first time they'd engaged in this behavior, he wanted it to be completely voluntary with no coercion. And, just as he'd suspected, she tasted sweet as honey. Her engorged clit throbbed against his tongue as he flicked and rubbed it with the strongest muscle in his body. Soon enough, he'd enter her and feel complete, but for the moment, it was all about her.

After a few minutes, he teased a finger inside her while his tongue continued playing with her clit, and he could tell by the way her thighs trembled and the way she began to pant that she was easing upon the edge of climax. He slowed his strokes then, hoping to draw it out longer, thereby making it even more explosive. It was then that he heard what sounded almost like a whimper in between the sharp breaths she was sucking into her lungs, as if she couldn't take much more.

He bore down with his tongue then, swirling it in a way that had driven women before her crazy. Her thighs began to quake rhythmically then, her knees grinding against his shoulders as he brought her home, one finger massaging that magical spot inside while his tongue relentlessly flicked her clit until she began crying out.

And, ah...there it was: music to his ears. "Oh, God, Brock. Oh, God. *Ohhhhhh, God...*"

He'd take it. She'd said his name once and, if she put him on a par with a deity, even better.

But no resting on his laurels. There was no stopping, not until she was completely satisfied. When her thighs slowed in their rhythmic quivering, he suckled the delicate firm flesh there before kissing his way back up her torso. "Don't think I'm done with you yet, Erica."

God, she was beautiful. Her mahogany eyes were half open, her body still tempting in its youthful pertness, desire still coming off her in waves. He knew now that even though he'd brought her to climax once, there was no telling how many times she had in her.

He wanted to find out.

He almost asked if she was ready for him to fill her, but he could tell from the look in her eyes that she was. He picked his jeans up off the floor and located his wallet, yanking a condom out of the center fold, grateful that he'd prepared for this moment. By the time he had his cock sheathed, Erica was practically pulling on him. Part of him wanted to flip her over and fuck her like a dog, letting her pussy grip his cock from that angle, but that would wait for another time.

What the fuck was he thinking? There would *be* no next time.

But his damn brains were gone. He slid his cock inside her, getting lost in that feeling of home, of warmth, of being where he belonged. And as her voice whispered his name once more before her pussy gripped his cock like she'd never let go, he fell the rest of the way to his complete and utter doom.

He was hers, now and forever.

CHAPTER FIFTEEN

UP UNTIL THIS very moment, Brock had thought the moments after sex were highly overrated. He wasn't into snuggling or cuddling or talking. Fuck that. It made women grow fonder and more apt to attachment. Instead, he'd always enjoyed the endorphin rush and often gave in to sleep.

Cuddling was for pussies.

But here he was, nestling Erica up against his chest and loving every fucking second of it. She was warm and soft and her room smelled like fresh fruit and flowers.

He could have slept there a week.

Lying to himself, he believed that every prolonged moment made it all the harder to leave, to *want* to leave. Every extra second he spent holding her made her more likely to become attached to him...and vice versa. No matter how amazing the sex was or how perfect this moment felt, he needed to get his ass out of there. *Now.*

She was not, nor would she ever be, his fiancée.

She was not his girlfriend.

He was not in love with her. And, even if he was, that wasn't part of the deal.

It was time to get the fuck out of there—and it was time to strap on a shield. He hadn't been guarding that which hadn't seemed to need protection, namely, his heart, and now it was too late. The best he could do would be to recover whatever little bit of himself he had left, hang onto it with all he had, and do his damnedest to come out unscathed.

That meant that Brock the asshole wasn't coming out to play. No...he was here to stay.

It was the only way.

Erica lay in her empty bed, unable to drift off to sleep. Two hardcore orgasms should have primed her for sweet nothingness, but Brock had left suddenly. At first, it had seemed as though he'd feathered his nest and planned to stay till morning but then, without warning, he said he had to leave, muttering something about preparing for court tomorrow as he pulled his shirt over his head.

Ah, it was just as well. She'd grown too used to his presence and, during their lovemaking, had all but forgotten the fiancé façade was just their grownup version of playing house. He was no more her betrothed than she was the next in line to run Ford & Associates. It just wasn't meant to be...not in the cards.

And, for some reason, although there were no promises broken nor vows failed, it disturbed her sleep all night long, and no amount of caffeine from Starbucks could touch the fatigue she felt the next day...but at least the level of tiredness matched the ache in her heart. Warranted or not, it saddened her that playtime with Brock was nearing its end, because he'd turned out to be the best boyfriend she could have ever wished for—even with all the things about himself that drove her crazy.

Her tune changed at work the next day, though. She'd seen him for all of five minutes before he rushed off to court, and he told her he'd look over any motions she prepared throughout the day when he got back. But he returned by eleven that morning, pissed off because the trial had been continued, something about the state needing to examine new evidence that would, of course, be shared with the defense should they choose to use it.

He was in a grouchy mood, though, sour and inconsolable, and Erica wondered if he was always this churlish when court didn't go his way. If so, maybe she needed to rethink the way her heart was swelling in her chest at the sight of this man.

But she'd been saying that over the past few days, especially since last night, trying to remind herself how stupid it was to let herself fall in love, to become attached to a man she could never have.

When she called Harriet, his secretary told her to wait until after lunch to see him. Usually, his crankiness wore off after a good meal. "Like a typical man," she said. Then, whispering, she added, "Just like my husband."

Erica didn't know if that made it better or worse.

But she waited and, when she came to Brock's office at one, Harriet told her he was expecting her. She entered the office and Brock was on speaker phone, having a war of words with a man she assumed was another attorney. Brock was pacing back and forth, occasionally barking toward the phone, but he waved her in and indicated that she needed to be quiet until he was done.

"When do I get copies of this new stuff?" he growled.

"I told you, Ford. We need to assess the validity first."

"And we couldn't go without it?"

There was a slight pause on the other end of the line. "Not if it's as important and it seems like it might be. Look…you know I'd give you the same courtesy."

Brock let out a brief *harrumph* before speaking. "I'm sure you would. See you in court." He pressed a button on his phone, hanging up, before asking, "And what can I do for you?"

Hmm. No sign of the warm man she'd engaged with in things both naughty and nice the night before. It was as if he'd switched bodies with an alien. Actually, this was more likely his usual self. Heavily sexed must have brought out the sweet in him.

The sex had been amazing…but obviously not worth it. She could *not* allow herself to fall in love with a Jekyll and Hyde.

Too late.

"I wondered if you could go over this motion for me? I think I've included everything I need but—"

He snatched the document out of her hands. It took everything she had to refrain from asking, *Rude much?* Turning one page after another, glancing quickly through the salient points, he said, "This is fine." Handing it back to her, he asked, "Where are the others?"

"What others?"

"The other motions for the other cases."

"I haven't actually written the mo—"

"Time is money, Larson," he barked. "A paralegal could have

all those motions typed up, ready for me to sign by now. What's the hold up?"

Her jaw wanted to hit the floor from shock. And then she felt a brief flash of hurt, but it helped her realize that, after all, she only had a business arrangement with Brock, nothing more. "You're supposed to be *training* me, you big jerk." She stomped toward the door. "But I guess I'll find a competent paralegal to help instead." Testing her theory, she added, "I'm pretty sure there are a couple of hot ones down on the first floor." And she left, firmly closing the door behind her, resisting the urge to slam it like she would have as a teenager.

Before actually storming off, she calmly marched back to the door and opened it, sliding her body in and shutting the door one more time, quietly enough that she hoped Harriet thought she was still in the office. With a quick clip, she made her way to the front of his desk and said, so calmly it was eerie, "I'm almost out of your hair, okay? This ride's almost done. If your dad officially calls it quit by Christmas, then you don't have much longer. I'd only ask that you treat me with a little respect while I'm still playing your fiancée." His eyes were wide but she saw that fucking amused twinkle in them. God, she wanted to slap his face so hard the twinkle wouldn't reappear till he was forty.

Shrugging, he said with no emotion, "Fine."

Erica couldn't help the tiny snort that communicated her disbelief and displeasure. "Fine," she repeated and made her way back across the room.

Yes, fine. That was good enough.

Thank goodness for Camilla. No matter how busy her friend was, she always had time to chat. Over the phone, her voice was high pitched but quiet enough that Erica could tell she was trying to keep the conversation from Gary's ears. "I can't believe you slept with him!"

"I can't either. But what's done is done."

"I suppose that adds to the realism of your little ruse, but it's going to make it harder for your heart to distinguish between fantasy and reality."

"Already there, my friend. Already there."

Camilla gasped. "You haven't—"

"Yes, and I know how stupid it is. Falling in love with Brock Ford, perpetual bachelor, is one of the stupidest things I ever allowed myself to do." Erica told her about how he'd seemed to alternate between hot and cold and then said, "So I don't know. Maybe he's feeling a little something for me, too? But that wasn't our agreement."

Camilla laughed. "It's not something either of you counted on. Give him some time. But…"

"But what?"

"When can I meet him?"

"Um…*never.*"

"No, seriously, Erica. I've got to meet the guy who captured my bestie's heart—even if she's going to demand it back."

"You're gonna hate him."

"No, I'm not."

"Yes, you are."

"You don't know that."

"I don't know how you can't. He's nothing like me."

"Then his qualities will complement yours."

Erica laughed then. "You're not going to take no for an answer, are you?"

"Nope. You can't always win the Stubborn Olympics, girlfriend."

She sighed. It seemed that everyone, Brock included, wanted to prolong the agony. Even her parents asked how he was doing every time they chatted on the phone; once in a while, they even asked in a text. There was no winning when it came to Brock. She just hated being the loser in this stupid match.

Brock had said he'd love to meet her friends. "All part of the game." He had no clue that Camilla knew their secret, and Erica was perfectly happy keeping it that way. Gary was in the dark, and that would likely make Camilla's acting more believable.

They met at seven thirty at a trendy restaurant downtown, one that required searching and paying well for good parking—but Brock managed to get a reservation for four. From the outside, the restaurant didn't look very big but it was like a cavern inside.

Brock held the door for Erica and she stepped inside a room that wasn't much brighter than the outdoors illuminated by street lights. As her eyes adjusted, though, she saw a hostess dressed in black with accents of white standing at a huge wooden podium in front of what looked like a mirrored hutch. Brock told her they had a reservation and she said their friends had already arrived and were seated in the bar.

She'd fetch them after seating the lovely couple.

They walked through a sea of young professionals who looked like they were unwinding after a long day—but they couldn't party too much, because tomorrow was Friday and would demand their continued attention. As Erica looked around at all the suits—on men and women alike—she was glad she'd chosen to wear a little black dress. Hers was a little different from the standard, and Brock had yet to see the whole thing, but the top, while long-sleeved, was lacy, and midback had a diamond-shaped cut from the bottom of her shoulder blades to just a few inches above her ass crack, making it slightly on the sexy side. Not that little black dresses needed much modification. But she'd also worn her hair down and anticipated having fun with her dear friend, whether or not their men were involved.

As always, Brock looked hot—suit without a tie, a little more form-fitting than his day wear. His facial hair was peeking through his skin, making him look a bit more rugged—and desirable, damn him. Erica could imagine alpha males hating him because he looked ready to take them all on without a word—and the sense was that he would win, so why bother?

After they were seated in the booth against the back wall, away from most of the frenetic activity of the yuppies bouncing back and forth from tables to bar and back again, Erica looked around. Across the room were huge windows facing the sidewalk and, although the traffic had eased up, there was still a steady stream of cars dashing down the street. On the wall were large framed abstract prints in monochrome, the dark grays and blacks matching the décor of the restaurant.

A few seconds later, the hostess was leading Camilla and Gary to the table. Camilla looked lovely as always in a light gray pantsuit with a bright yellow blouse, making Erica feel like Cam was telling nature, "Fine, winter's here, but it's always spring in my heart." She stood to hug her friend and felt Brock sliding out of the booth seat behind her, but she saw him shaking hands with Gary before she gave him a hug as well.

Gary's outfit was simple like Camilla's, only he wore a black sweater with dark gray slacks. Erica noticed that he was as tall as Brock, but his blond hair contrasted with her fake fiancé's darker locks. Brock's hair was part of what made him sexy.

No. She had to stop that.

Brock wasn't interested in her as a girlfriend, wife, or real fiancée—he was only interested in how she could help him move into the position he wanted by pretending to be his betrothed, and she knew, no matter how real it *seemed* at times, it was all just make believe. So thinking Brock was handsome, sexy, witty, charming, good in bed—all that shit was off the table.

That also meant that, aside from the most superficial pretense with her pretend fiancé this evening, she was free to focus on her best friend and the food. Brock did not require anything else from her...nor would he get it.

Erica was the only one at the table who knew everyone there, so she asked them all to introduce themselves. Once that was done, Brock asked if anyone would mind if he took the liberty to order a bottle of wine—"unless," he said, "anyone is planning on eating red meat."

No one cared and Brock ordered something he promised would go well with anything fish or fowl. So everyone perused the menu and, when the waitress stopped by, she took their orders. Shortly thereafter, a man in a tux came by with a bottle of wine in a bucket that he placed beside the table. After opening it, he poured them each a glass and then left.

"Brock, just so you know, Camilla is my closest, dearest friend, and because I don't ever see that changing, I thought you should meet her."

Her friend giggled. "Well, that and I demanded to meet the man who captured my bestie's heart!"

Camilla was playing it just right—not too pushy or overly dramatic, but cute and sweet. Brock fell for it, and Erica was grateful for that, because she imagined he often had to assess the veracity of certain people on the stand. Then again, he wasn't expecting to meet any liars tonight, so he might have been off guard—and that was fine.

"I am a very lucky man," Brock said, turning his head and

kissing Erica on the temple.

She felt like digging her three-inch heel into his foot or kicking him underneath the table. He was so full of shit, it wasn't even funny—and she was nearing the end of her rope. Instead, she smiled as warmly as she could muster and leaned her head against his shoulder, hoping it looked loving.

Of course, Gary was the only person she had to convince...since Camilla already knew. And the way her friend smiled at her, Erica nearly lost it, because Cam was actually holding two secrets instead of one—not just Brock's but Erica's as well, the one of falling in love with the man who didn't deserve her.

Probably eager to change the subject, Brock asked, "What is it you do for a living, Gary?"

"I'm a software developer. When I first got into computers as a kid, I always imagined myself in a job surrounded by them—and I am—but it's not nearly as exciting as I'd thought back then...and it's also not just about computers. We're talking phones, videogame systems, and other things you'd never think of."

Brock nodded, sipping his wine, and then Erica said, "And Camilla works for the same company, but in marketing."

"Ah, do I dare ask the company?"

Camilla laughed. "Not in public!"

Erica couldn't quite read the look on Gary's face. It was one of concern, confusion, and doubt, and she had no idea what that meant. "What is it *you* do, Brock?"

"I'm the son of Brady Ford of Ford & Associates. I'm a partner—as are my brothers—but my father is getting ready to hand the entire practice over to us soon."

Gary raised an eyebrow, but he now wore a mask, as if he was hiding his emotions. "So you practice law?"

Brock, ever charming, smiled. "Every chance I get."

Setting down his wine glass, Gary asked, "Do you happen to remember a man by the name of Judd Fleming?"

"Hmm. That name seems a little familiar but I don't know why. Is that someone I should know?"

The waitress popped up for just a moment, long enough to deliver the appetizer. Instead of getting salads, they'd opted for little chicken bites with a variety of sweet and spicy sauces for dipping. Camilla asked if any of the sauces had nuts in them because of an allergy and, once the waitress assured her all the sauces were nut free, she was on her way and everyone grabbed a piece of chicken and began dunking.

Brock asked if Gary was into sports and Camilla's fiancé admitted that he had a weakness for pro football—so he was enjoying himself right now. Camilla rolled her eyes as if telling Brock, *Thanks a lot*, but she smiled and it gave Erica a chance to chitchat about stupid stuff for a few minutes.

But after the meal arrived, a sort of reverent hush fell over the table. The food was presented more exquisitely than Erica was used to. It was so beautiful, in fact, that all four seemed to want to admire it before eating. Finally, though, Erica said, "I'm doing this." Camilla followed suit before the guys joined in.

Halfway through the meal, the wine settling and the food filling like it should, Gary repeated an earlier, seemingly forgotten, question. "So, Brock, I can't remember what you said. Did you say, yes, you remember Judd Fleming?"

Brock shook his head, cutting into the last of the tilapia on his plate. "The name tickles something in my brain, but I don't remember anyone specifically."

"He's a cop. He *was* a detective, with the force for over a decade."

Brock nodded. "And how do you know him?"

"He's my cousin."

"Why do you think *I* know him?"

Gary's forehead creased in a frown before he answered. "There was a trial several years ago. A kid—some punk—stole something from a pawn shop and Judd was on patrol in the neighborhood. The kid had just jumped out the window when Judd came around the corner, but the kid ran down the alley. Judd cornered him and the kid pulled out a gun—so, after telling the kid to drop the gun twice, Judd fired."

Brock raised an eyebrow. "It's coming back to me. The *kid*—Theodore Walton was his name—had a gun in his hand, but it wasn't loaded."

"It was a gun he'd stolen from the pawn shop, one that linked him to another crime."

Brock nodded. "I remember."

"Well, do you happen to remember how you grilled Judd? Tore him up one side and down the other on the witness stand? Humiliated him?"

Erica could honestly say she'd never seen Gary this bent out of shape about anything before. Granted, she didn't know him that well, but he didn't seem to be the kind of guy to go overboard. He was genuinely upset, though, and she wanted to hear her pretend fiancé's explanation.

"I did what I always do. I questioned him."

"*Badgered* him is more like it."

"Look…Gary. I am sworn to defend my clients to the best of my abilities. I don't half ass it. It doesn't matter who I think is innocent or guilty. I have to do my best to represent my client."

"And just how did that guy wind up getting *you* as an attorney anyway? Don't you charge a pretty penny?"

"My father has always made my brothers and me take at least one pro bono case a year. Theo just happened to be my lucky guy."

"And Judd the unlucky one." Gary set his fork down on his plate with enough force that it made a loud clinking noise. Erica hoped he continued to keep his cool, but he felt like a volcano ready to blow. "Did you know my cousin takes antidepressants now? And he pushes papers today. He can't bring himself to work a beat anymore. He even sees a therapist."

Brock threw his napkin on the table and pushed his plate away. "And how's that my problem, Gary? I was just doing my job."

"So was Judd. He's an honest guy trying to protect the citizens of Colorado and—"

"Look…you seem like a decent enough guy. I could go over all the particulars of the case if you wanted. I could go back to the office, dredge up the file, go over the minutia. I doubt you know the whole story but I can tell you this—if your cousin is still grappling with that trial from years ago, maybe he shouldn't have become a cop. Maybe he's not suited for that line of work."

Gary's face and neck had turned a shade of pink that was just this side of red, and Erica began to feel frightened that he might ask Brock to step outside—not that the man didn't deserve it. He sounded more like a callous asshole than she'd ever heard from him before and she was feeling more than a little repulsed at the moment.

Gary stood. "I think I need to leave, Camilla. I hate to do that, because I know you haven't seen Erica in a while—"

"No, it's okay."

"Sorry, Erica," he said, addressing her directly. "I know you and Cammy are close, but I *cannot* go to your wedding. It's the principle of the thing."

Why the hell did Erica feel so embarrassed? It wasn't like she was really going to marry Brock.

Just because her heart had fallen for him...

She simply nodded while Camilla said, "I'll call you tomorrow, okay?" She gave another bob of her head but she was feeling a little speechless.

Gary looked at Erica one last time. "My bosses are always looking for an on-staff lawyer or two. If you decide you're tired of working for a family with questionable ethics, let me know and I'll put in a good word for you. You'll probably do half the work for twice the pay—and you'll be able to sleep at night." He threw down several bills before he and Camilla sped out of the restaurant.

Brock grabbed the wine bottle and drained what was left into his glass. "Want some?" Erica shook her head while Brock guzzled the drink that was meant to be savored. "Well...that was a little awkward."

Yeah...

"You not talking anymore?"

"I don't know what to say, Brock."

"There's nothing to say, except that your friend doesn't get it. I'm not paid to be emotional or care. I'm paid to do a job—one that a lot of other people don't like to do."

"You seem to like it all right."

The waitress stopped by the table with a tray full of decadent pastries, cheesecake slices, and chocolatey concoctions. "Dessert?" She tilted her head. "There were four of you, right?"

Erica nodded. Brock turned to her and asked, "Want anything?"

"No. I think I want to go home now."

He frowned but said, "Just the check, please." Then he turned to Erica. "You're going to have to get a thicker skin, babe. This job's not easy and it's not for everyone."

"You can be a lawyer and not defend bad guys, Brock."

"Someone's gotta do it, Erica. Might as well be me."

Like a petulant child, she wanted to tell him she was ready to go home, that she no longer wished to play house anymore, but they were at the waitress' mercy. Soon enough, she brought the check on a flimsy piece of white thermal paper. Brock pulled out his credit card while the waitress cleared a few dishes and promised to be right back.

Erica could sense that Brock, being no idiot, knew she was upset with him and she didn't care. She couldn't understand how someone could turn his humanity off and on like that. How could he seem sweet and loveable one minute, a monster the next? What was she missing?

In her heart, she knew the answer. This man, the one who'd destroyed the cop named Judd Fleming, the one who'd unapologetically told his cousin it was all in a day's work, the one who was lying to his parents about a sham engagement just so he could get his fair piece of the pie—*that* was the real Brock. And so the guy she *thought* she was in love with—he was a figment of her imagination.

Rather, he was a crafted version of a better self that Brock had no intention of becoming. And Erica had just exposed her heart to him—for no good reason and certainly no good outcome.

Once the bill was paid, they made their way out of the cavernous restaurant, not talking, not discussing, because there was nothing to say. Erica didn't wait for Brock to hold the door for her, instead storming out before he could get there. She wouldn't have much of a choice when they got to the car, because he'd need to unlock it first, but she was making a statement. By the time they were on the road and he was driving Erica back to her apartment, he said, "It's easy to point fingers when you've never been in that position. When you defend a person accused of a crime, Erica, you have to do everything in your power to save their skin. You exploit the weaknesses of the other party. In that particular case, if I recall correctly, Fleming had just had another questionable incident happen at work a month or so earlier, one involving a gun. I don't think all cops are bad guys, honey, and I don't think Fleming necessarily was, but I did wonder—out loud—if he should have been on the streets. Had he never had to enter a courtroom, I wouldn't have had to assess his competency as a cop, but as my client's attorney, I had to put him through the wringer. So I did."

Erica could no longer hold her tongue. "But what did you say that made him lose his zeal for his job? It sounds like the guy's just a shell now."

"I just hold up a mirror, Erica. If they don't like the reflection, it's their problem."

Well…she was being forced to look at her own reflection now and she didn't much like it—and she had a few decisions to grapple with before the sun came up.

CHAPTER SIXTEEN

BROCK HADN'T SLEPT a wink throughout the night, and it was because of that stupid little thing called a *conscience*. The damn thing had never bothered him before, so what the hell was the point now?

Of all the words Erica's friend Gary had said last night, the ones that had stuck with Brock the most were when he'd told Erica she could come work for his company so she could sleep better at night. He'd scoffed at those words last night but this morning? Not so much.

He knew two things were part of the equation at the moment. The first was that he'd never viewed Fleming the cop as a human being before. That perspective was a skill he'd had to acquire and hone, because viewing the other side as people with feelings made him less of a shark with killer instincts. The second was pretty fucking stupid...but it was that he hated disappointing Erica. To see how disgusted she looked wrecked him.

But throughout the night, he'd grappled with all those things and, though he was exhausted by four-thirty that morning, he knew what he had to do to make all things right. Whether or not it was too late to recapture Erica's heart was immaterial. And whether or not his father approved didn't matter. It was time to practice his craft in a new way—and if that didn't fit with his firm's goals, maybe *he'd* ask Gary for that corporate lawyer position.

But, first, he had a few things to rectify...

*   *   *

Erica awoke to dreary gray skies. By the time she left her apartment, she could tell that flakes were going to start falling sometime throughout the day, but for now some kind of storm had stalled overhead and was camping out, keeping the city dark, foreboding, and gloomy—and why not? It matched the dreariness of her heart.

But she knew what she had to do now. She put on a black pantsuit and, in spite of her mood, paired it with a pink blouse, and she arrived at work early. First, she went to Brock's office, because she'd intended to break the news to him before anyone else—but he wasn't there. Harriet said Brock had told her he would be in later than usual, but he wasn't in court that day. She wasn't sure where he was, but he was the boss, so he made the rules.

"Can I leave something for him in his office?"

"Of course."

Had Harriet known what Erica planned to leave, she might have questioned it.

Then Erica spent the next two hours packing up her office and getting it ready for whomever would pick up where she left off. She organized the case files she'd been working on, writing long notes as to what she'd done so that any of the paralegals or other attorneys could pick up where she left off without having to backtrack or sift through information too much.

She sipped another cup of coffee, gazing out her third-story window to see the first few flakes falling from the fluffy clouds hanging low. Once her cup was drained, she headed to Brock's office one last time in hopes of catching him, but he still wasn't there. She sent him a text then, letting him know that she was giving her notice and, since he wasn't around, she was going to give it to his dad. She'd wanted him to be a part of it but she wasn't going to wait all day.

She'd made up her mind and now it was time to act.

As an afterthought, she added, *I hope things work out for you, your family, and the future of the firm, but I can no longer work for you. I'm leaving the ring on your desk.*

She was past judging or examining, but she needed to do something for her life for good—and she now knew that Ford & Associates was not the place for it, so it was time to move on.

What came next in her life? She didn't know. She was pretty sure she wanted to keep her apartment, stay in the big city, do good things here, but her job was going to be elsewhere.

Dropping the cell phone in her purse that sat in the big bottom drawer of her desk, she stood, smoothing back her hair, and then grabbed the folded piece of paper off her desk before walking into the big hallway. Brady Ford's office was to the right at the end of the hall, taking up most of that side of the building. She'd never been in there but had heard rumors and, after sitting in Bret's office many a time and dropping her jaw at the expanse, she had no idea what to expect from Daddy Ford's office. Hell, she didn't even know if he would see her—but it was a chance she had to take. She'd fretted and considered talking to Bret, her old boss, but finally decided that only the guy in charge of the whole shebang would do. It didn't matter that he was giving up the reins sometime in the near future. He was the big guy right now and so he was the man she needed to speak with.

The man's secretary was probably considering retirement as well, Erica thought as she approached the woman with the giant desk, computer, and old-fashioned typewriter tucked on a side table. However, the woman knew her own importance and she eyed Erica over the top of her glasses as if scrutinizing everything about her.

Talk about feeling like you were under a magnifying glass...

"Can I help you?"

Why this woman intimidated Erica, she didn't know. All she could figure was it was because she was nervous about what she was about to do. But she mustered up every last bit of confidence she felt before opening her mouth. "I wondered if I could talk with Mr. Ford for a few moments."

His secretary arched an eyebrow. "Do you have an appointment?"

Of course—because, if she'd learned *anything* from Brock over the past couple of months, it was that *time was money*. The time she would take with Brady Ford would not be billable—and, therefore, not important, according to the firm's standards. "It won't take much time, but—"

Bret opened the door to his father's office from the inside, dark brown coffee mug in hand, and said, "Erica, what a pleasant surprise. Ever since Brock stole you away from me, I've hardly

173

gotten to see you."

What? Was this her former boss? Had he ever treated her this warmly before?

She forced herself to smile and said, "I know. It's been a while."

"So what are you doing in this neck of the woods?"

Ha. So she wasn't going to have to go through the gatekeeper—if she was lucky. "I was hoping to talk to your father for a few minutes."

"What about? Anything I can help with?"

Might as well be honest. "Um...my future with the firm...and the wedding."

Bret raised his eyebrows and got a clue. Nodding, he said, "I think that can be arranged. Mind if I sit in, considering dad's handing the firm over to us soon?"

"No, that's fine," especially if it meant she'd get the audience *now*.

Bret peeked his head in the door. "Dad, got a few more minutes?"

"Yes, son."

Opening the door farther, he said, "Erica is here to see us."

"Ah, Erica. So nice to see you," the elder Ford said, standing up, his hands outstretched to greet her. "If only *all* my daughters-in-law wished to practice law. What a firm we'd have."

Well...he was in for a major disappointment.

"Please...have a seat." Erica was pretty sure the secretary was possibly seething now because not only did she get an audience with Mr. Ford, but she got a front row seat, and the man didn't seem to be in any huge hurry to get her out of there.

Unfortunately, she didn't feel up to visiting for too terribly long. Brady Ford, looking like a sweet and kindly man she might see in the park hunting around for a chess partner—except in a suit and tie instead of a sweater and jaunty cap—said, "What can I do for you today?"

Erica inhaled a deep breath, as if to fortify herself, and then she blew it out. Bret, a joking tone in his voice, noticed and said, "That sounds pretty serious."

Erica nodded. "Actually, it kind of is." How could she word this so that she could keep her end of the bargain—of keeping her supposed fiancé's secret safe? Just because Brock had no integrity didn't mean she didn't. Yes, she'd participated in the deception of his family but now she regretted it, because—overall, in spite of their foibles and despite her own distrust of wealthy folks—they seemed like decent enough people. And, while she thought making sure every client had a decent attorney who worked hard for them was a noble idea, Brock had seemed to cross a line somewhere and she wasn't sure where that was. In a way, that was frightening, and she didn't want to start sliding down that slippery slope. Erica most definitely knew the kind of lawyer she wanted to be—and Brock wasn't teaching her that.

And, although she knew they'd let her, she definitely didn't want to go back to doing nothing but research. *Ugh.*

"I'm not sure where to start...except to say that I don't think my employment here with Ford & Associates is working out."

The elder Mr. Ford asked, "Why not? Is there something that's not working for you?"

"Well—"

"We can't afford to lose a mind as sharp as yours. If you're concerned about any wayward accusations of nepotism, we can quash them. In fact, we can completely separate you and Brock so as to avoid even the appearance of any type of favoritism."

"I appreciate that, sir, but that's not all of it."

"Oh?"

Bret had hardly spoken a word, but he was definitely rapt in her words.

"Uh...about Brock..."

And what would she even say about him?

"Brock is—"

The intercom buzzed and Mr. Ford said, "I'm sorry. One moment."

He pushed on a button and the hollow sounding voice came through the speakers. "Brock said he needs to speak with—wait!"

His secretary's voice continued, wavering between yelling and trying to stay calm, as Brock himself burst through the door, also not waiting for the almighty gatekeeper secretary to hand him the key.

Brady raised both eyebrows and crossed his hands in front of him on the desk. Erica couldn't help but notice an amused twinkle in the older man's eyes. "Ah, my son. Why do I get the feeling you know why your fiancée is here?"

Brock barely looked at his father and then Bret, as if his eyes could apologize—but that was exactly what he was trying to do. "Erica, I just need five minutes before you do anything rash."

"Too late."

"No, it's not too late. You're not out the door yet...so, please, give me five minutes."

Giving him what he asked for was a stupid idea—and yet she felt compelled by this charismatic devilish man. She sighed and then said, "Fine—but no playing Mr. Defense Attorney with me. You try it once and I'm out of here."

His genuine eyes quelled her suspicions. "Last night...what you said really resonated with me. You shined a harsh light inside my soul, Erica, exposing all my demons, all my dark secrets—and it was ugly. Sometimes, I'm *too* good at my job and it's at the expense of others.

"So when I got up this morning, I did a little research—and instead of coming to the office, I met Judd Fleming." Erica raised her eyebrows but let him continue talking. "Like your friend said last night, he's working a desk at the PD—and, at first, he refused to see me, but I managed to meet with him. He still had a lot of anger—toward *me*—but we had a long talk and, whether he forgave me or not, I apologized."

Erica wasn't convinced nor impressed. "Good for you. Your karma score is no doubt better." She took a deep breath before adding, "And how do we know you're not just saying that? We have no way to verify your claims."

Brock's classic smirk lit up his face. Dammit, he was still so good looking, it made her stomach muscles clench. "Actually, you do. See, Judd and I went out for breakfast, and I felt so bad, like I'd ruined the man...but somehow we moved past all the anger and frustration and just talked like two men resolving a grievance should—and I wound up hiring him to be a full-time investigator for Ford & Associates."

That was when Brock's father stepped in. "Wait a minute, son. You didn't consult your brothers or me before making this decision."

Brock turned and said, "Dad, we've contracted out for as long as I can remember, essentially paying piece rate to whatever guy we could find to do the job. If you've got someone on salary, they can do whatever you need whenever you need it. You're getting ready to hand the firm over to us, so I made an executive decision based upon the future needs of the firm." He took a breath, radiating confidence. "If you still disagree, I'll pay him out of my own pocket."

After a long pause, Brady Ford smiled, the crinkles beside his eyes deepening before he chuckled. "Ah, a decision maker. I respect that, son. Being able to make decisions for the good of the firm is part of why I ultimately broke away and hung my own shingle all those years ago. I trust your judgment. Why don't we put him on the payroll next week?"

"I thought you'd say that—but he needs more time than that. Two weeks' notice to the department before he comes over here."

"Ah, of course."

Well, all this familial bonding and ass kissing was nice, but Erica had made a decision and it was time to get out of here. "Brock, I'm glad you've finally had a pang of conscience, and I hope it stays with you as you continue practicing law. But I was just tendering my resignation to your father."

"But why, Erica? If it's just because of me...I'm a good man, Erica. I just made a bad decision or two...but you've made me realize I can do my job and still do what's right."

"Good for you, Brock. But I—"

He must have known she was going to tell him she was "breaking up" with him—but if he wanted to handle it instead, that was fine. This was his game, his ruse, and he was the one who had to live with his family when it was all over. So long as she could leave unscathed, she would leave quietly.

Brock got down on a knee again, like he had at his father's retirement gala over a month ago, but instead of looking at Erica, he turned his head to talk to his father and brother. "I have a bit of a confession to make. A couple of months ago, I convinced Erica to pretend to be my fiancée, because I thought it would help my chances of being a full partner in the firm when you retired, dad—all your speeches about being a family man sunk in with us, and not only hadn't I found the right woman, but I wasn't ready to settle down."

He turned to Erica then. "But the past several weeks with you have opened my eyes and changed my mind. You, Erica Larson, are funny, sweet, intelligent—and you challenge me like no other woman ever has. I would be a damn idiot to let you go."

Erica felt her heart swell and her eyes fill as his words flooded her heart...because that meant he loved her back. It was something she'd shut herself off from this morning but, hearing his words, she let the walls inside her heart fall down and absorb all he was saying.

Before she could answer, he turned his head to his father again. "I was being deceptive and dishonest. I lied to you...and so if that means you no longer want me here at Ford & Associates, I'll go somewhere else." He swallowed but kept talking before either his father or oldest brother could speak. "After finding Erica, this work doesn't hold the fascination for me that it once did. Do I want to continue practicing law? Yes, of course, but now it all pales in comparison." He turned to her once more. "Go if you must. Leave if you can't find a place in your heart for me—but go knowing I love you and want you in my life."

How the hell could any woman say no to that? "Oh, Brock..."

"I'm taking that as a yes," he said, taking her left hand and sliding the ring back on her finger. Erica looked down at the glittery jewelry, loving it all the more now, because now it felt like it belonged. When she looked up into Brock's eyes, he stroked her cheek and then kissed her.

It was more magical than ever.

Then Brock stood, Erica's hand in his, and she joined him. He said to his father, "I understand if you need me to leave, dad, but don't make her go. She's a brilliant—"

Brady Ford began laughing then, an infectious hearty chortle that had them all chuckling before he spoke. "Son, you've always been good with sleight of hand, and you're an expert when it comes to making people see things the way you want them to. It's what's made you not just a skillful defense attorney but a strong litigator in general.

"You know my philosophies about marriage and how it makes you a better lawyer, yes, but I wanted to give my firm to *all* my sons, married or not." Brady looked at Erica then and said, "But you *would* be a damn fool to let this young lady go. You might have just figured out you're in love with her, but the rest of us have seen it all along. I think you're perfect for my son, Ms. Larson, and I would be proud to call you my daughter-in-law—and one of the brightest attorneys at my firm."

That Bret also smiled and nodded told Erica everything she needed to know. She *was* part of the family—all she had to do was say yes.

So she did.

And Brock kissed her again, holding her close.

When they left his father's office, though, his arm around her waist, she needed to be absolutely certain. Away from any stray ears, she whispered, "This is *real*, right? We're not continuing this charade...we're *really* engaged?"

Brock started laughing and picked her up in his arms so that her feet no longer touched the ground, twirling her around. "Yes, I really want you to be my wife. You gave me a real yes, didn't you?"

She smiled then and touched her nose to his. "Yes. I love you, Brock."

"I love you, too, Erica. And even though I wasn't able to prepare the most eloquent argument for your hand that I'm capable of, I hope you believe it."

"I do—with all my heart." And it wouldn't be long before she said *I do* once more, this time for forever.

EPILOGUE

"WHAT'S THE TEMPERATURE there right now, dad?"

"You don't really want to know, do you?"

Erica's mother chimed in. "It's two degrees here."

Brock smiled as he walked through the door, hearing his new bride on a Skype conversation with her parents. "What about you? What's the temperature there?"

"Last I checked, it was in the mid-seventies."

"Oh, what a shame," her dad teased.

"You're just jealous," her mother said, and Brock entered the bedroom area of their suite, bag in one hand, paper cup in the other.

Erica looked up from the laptop sitting on the coffee table and gazed into his eyes. He would swear this woman had become more beautiful since he'd proposed for real. She was more than a sight for sore eyes—she'd become his whole world, and nothing would ever be the same. And that was a good thing.

"Oh! Is that what I think it is?"

He grinned. *Score!* "It's true. Starbucks is *everywhere.*"

Her mother's voice came through the computer. "He's definitely got your number."

Erica cocked an eyebrow. "Well, let's see. What's in the cup, mister?"

"White mocha latte—and they asked if you wanted it hot. I said yes."

Grinning, she said, "Oh, you're a keeper!"

"I got us a little breakfast, too."

"We'll let you go, honey. So glad you're enjoying your honeymoon."

"It's the best." She blew kisses at the computer screen. "Love you guys."

"Love you, too."

Brock bent over and waved at them before Erica closed the window. She stood up and wrapped her arms around him, kissing him on the cheek. "What did I ever do to deserve you?"

"It's me who should be asking that question." After kissing her like it was the last time he would ever taste her lips, he said, "I got us some breakfast, if you want it."

Erica put on a fake grimace and said, "Uh, no way. You're already gonna make me run a mile on the beach. I don't want to make it two."

"Breakfast is the most important meal of the day."

She started laughing. Ah, he would never grow tired of the sound of her amusement. His heart swelled with gratitude. Not only had this woman opened up a part of him he hadn't known still existed, a part last seen in the fourth grade when he'd defended a school acquaintance from the playground bully, but she'd opened his eyes to love and all its possibilities. He was a richer man for it...and now, although he loved work, it was no longer his whole world.

Everything out there was open to him.

And with that realization dawning—and before his father officially retired—they chose Valentine's Day as their wedding day. The entire family—mother, brothers, and sisters-in-law—all thought it was a great idea, although Lisa was a little saddened that she couldn't help with the wedding, considering it was a quiet, fast wedding on the beach with two strangers serving as witnesses. To appease Lisa, though, Erica said they'd love to have a reception sometime in the spring, and her new sister-in-law could handle the whole thing. After all, she'd said, her side of the family would want to celebrate, too.

The wedding and honeymoon in Hawaii were ten days—and, now that they'd been there for five, Brock was beginning to think they should have taken a month. They'd have to come back again for a vacation and soon...and he would forever associate this place with his lovely bride.

For now, though, he wanted to consummate their union once more.

"I haven't had my workout yet, though. I'm thinking we could get in a little exercise before we eat."

Erica cocked a brown eyebrow, and just that look made his blood begin to swirl, all of it wanting to congregate in his eager member. "Are you thinking exercise between the sheets, handsome?"

"I thought you'd never ask." As his erection grew, he pressed it into her, kissing her again.

"And *that*, Mr. Ford, is why I haven't actually run along the beach with you yet. We spend too much time in bed."

"You say that like it's a *bad* thing, Mrs. Ford."

"That's *Larson*-Ford, mister…and if you want to ravish me, you'd better do it now before that white mocha latte begs me for attention."

Brock started laughing and literally swept her off her feet and into his arms. Breakfast? A jog along the beach? Coffee? They could all wait.

But making his new bride feel eternally loved couldn't. So he was off to rock her world and then cradle her in his arms like there was no tomorrow—because there wouldn't be if it wasn't for her.

BOOKS BY JADE C. JAMISON

Dream Guy

All I Want for Christmas is the Hot Guy in the Santa Suit

Picture Perfect

Charade

Heat

To Save Him

Savage

Substitute Boyfriend

Finger Bang

Quickies: Sexy Short Stories and Other Stuff

Old House

Then Kiss Me

MADversary

Laid Bare

Fabric of Night

Crossing the Line

TANGLED WEB SERIES

1 Tangled Web: A Steamy Heavy Metal Novella

2 Everything But

Punctured, Bruised, and Barely Tattooed (companion novel)

3 Seal All Exits

BULLET SERIES

1 Bullet: An Epic Rock Star Novel

2 Rock Bottom

3 Feverish

4 Fully Automatic

4.5 Christmas Stalkings

5 Slash and Burn

6 Locked and Loaded

FEVERISH SERIES

1 Feverish

1.5 Boiling Point

2 Scorched

NICKI SOSEBEE SERIES

1 Got the Life

2 Dead

3 No Place to Hide

4 Right Now

5 One More Time

6 Lost

7 Innocent Bystander

8 Blind

9 Fake

10 Lies

11 Dead Bodies Everywhere

CODIE SNOW SERIES

1 Fool Me Once

WISHES SERIES

1 Be Careful What You Wish For

VAGABONDS TRILOGY

1 On the Run
2 On the Road
3 On the Rocks

NONFICTION

Indie Writer Companion

ABOUT THE AUTHOR

For years, Jade C. Jamison tried really hard to write what she thought was more "literary" fiction, but she found herself compelled to write what you read by her today--sometimes gritty, raw, realistic stories and other times humorous, light tales--but most of the stories she writes revolve around relationships and characters finding their way through life. While she doesn't confine herself to just one genre, nor is there a nice neat label for what she writes, most of her work could be called erotic romance. Her main writing passions include rock star romance, romantic comedy, and romantic suspense.

She lives in Colorado with her husband and four children.

Find out more at www.jadecjamison.com
Sign up for Jade's newsletter at
http://www.subscribepage.com/JadeCJamison